THE COLLECTED WORKS OF BERNARD MALAMUD

THE TENANTS

THE COLLECTED WORKS OF BERNARD MALAMUD

DUBIN'S LIVES
REMBRANDT'S HAT
THE TENANTS
PICTURES OF FIDELMAN
THE FIXER
IDIOTS FIRST
A NEW LIFE
THE MAGIC BARREL
THE ASSISTANT
THE NATURAL

THE
TENANTS

BERNARD
MALAMUD

1981

CHATTO & WINDUS

LONDON

Published by
Chatto & Windus Ltd
40 William IV Street
London WC2N 4DF

First published in Great Britain in 1972
This edition published 1981

British Library Cataloguing in Publication
Data
Malamud, Bernard
The tenants.
I. Title
813'.54[F]   PS3563.A4
ISBN 0-7011-2451-2

Printed in the United States of America

For Janna

"Alive and with his eyes open he calls us his murderers."

ANTIPHON
Tetralogies

"I got to make it, I got to find the end . . ."

BESSIE SMITH

The Tenants

LESSER CATCHING SIGHT OF HIMSELF in his lonely glass wakes to finish his book. He smelled the living earth in the dead of winter. In the distance mournful blasts of a vessel departing the harbor. Ah, if I could go where it's going. He wrestles to sleep again but can't, unease like a horse dragging him by both bound legs out of bed. I've got to get up to write, otherwise there's no peace in me. In this regard I have no choice. "My God, the years." He flings aside the blanket and standing unsteadily by the loose-legged chair that holds his clothes slowly draws on his cold pants. Today's another day.

Lesser dresses unwillingly, disappointing surprise, because he had gone to bed in a fire of desire to write in the morning. His thoughts were sweet, impatient for tomorrow. He goes to sleep in anticipation and wakes resistant, mourning. For what? Whom? What useless dreams intervene? Though he remembers none although his sleep is stuffed with dreams, Lesser

reveries one touched with fear: Here's this stranger
I meet on the stairs.

"Who you looking for, brother?"

"Who you callin brother, mother?"

Exit intruder. Yesterday's prowler or already today's? Levenspiel in disguise? A thug he's hired to
burn or blow up the joint?

It's my hyperactive imagination working against the
grain. Lesser makes things hard for himself for certain reasons. That's a long tale but right now it means
he doesn't know how to end his book. Nor why the ending, this time, is so hard to come by if you've invented
every step that leads to it, though some crumble when
you look hard at them. Still, it's bound to come, it always has. Maybe it's some kind of eschatological
dodge? Like an end is more than I can stand? Each
book I write nudges me that much closer to death?

As soon as he ends one he begins another.

Now that the imagination is imagining Lesser imagines it done, the long labor concluded at last. Relief,
calm, mornings in bed for a month. Dawn on the sea,
rose lighting the restless waves touching an island
waking, breathing the fresh breath of its trees, flowers,
bayberry bushes, seashells. Ah, the once more sensuous smells of land surrounded by the womanly sea.
Birds rise from the shore, wheel, fly above the ragged,
mast-like palms into the lucent sky. Gulls mewling,

sudden storms of blackbirds shrilling over the violet water. Ah, this live earth, this sceptered isle on a silver sea, this Thirty-first Street and Third Avenue. This forsaken house. This happy unhappy Lesser having to write.

○

On this cold winter morning when the rusty radiator knocked like a hearty guest but gave off feeble warmth, yesterday's snow standing seven stiff inches on the white street, through which indigenous soot seeped, Harry Lesser, a serious man, strapped his time-piece on his wrist—time also lived on his back—and ran down six dirty flights of the all-but-abandoned, year 1900, faded bulky brick tenement he lived and wrote in. Thirty-five families had evacuated it in the nine months after demolition notices had been mailed but not Lesser, he hung on. Crossing Third against the light, feeling in the street's slush that he had left his rubbers under the sink, Harry, in wet sneakers, popped into a grocery store for his bread, milk, and half dozen apples. As he trotted home he glanced peripherally left and right, then cagily back to see whether his landlord or one of his legal henchmen was hanging around in somebody's wet doorway or crouched behind a snow-roofed car, laying for Lesser. A wasted thought because what could they do but once more try to persuade, and in this matter he is not persuasible. Levenspiel wants him out of the building so he can demolish it and put up another but Levenspiel he holds by the balls. The building was rent-controlled, and from the District Rent Office—they knew him well—Harry had learned he was a statutory tenant with certain useful rights. The others had accepted the landlord's payoff but Lesser stayed on and would for a time so he could finish his book where it was born. Not sentiment, he lived on habit; it saves time. Letting go of Levenspiel's frozen nuts he raced home in the snow.

Home is where my book is.

○

In front of the decaying brown-painted tenement, once a decent house, Lesser's pleasure dome, he gave it spirit—stood a single dented ash can containing mostly his crap, thousands of torn-up screaming words and rotting apple cores, coffee grinds, and broken eggshells, a literary rubbish can, the garbage of language become the language of garbage. Emptied twice weekly without request; he was grateful. Along the street in front of the house ran a pedestrian pathway through the unshoveled snow. No super for months, gone like a ghost. The heat was automatically controlled, on the sparse side for the lone inhabitant on the top floor, for the last three and a half months Robinson Crusoe up there, the thermostat set in the cellar's bowels by Levenspiel himself. If it pooped out, and it pooped often—the furnace had celebrated its fiftieth birthday—you called the complaint number of Rent and Housing Maintenance, who bedeviled Himself; and in a few hours, if not more, it reluctantly came back on, thanks to the janitor in the pockmarked imitation-Reformation gray job across the street who poked around when Levenspiel begged him on the telephone. Just enough heat to be cold. You saw your inspired breath. Harry had a heater in his study to keep his fingers fluent in the dead of winter, not bad although noisy and costs for electricity. Things could be worse and had been, but he was still a writer writing. Rewriting. That was his forte, he had lots to change—true, too, in his life. Next building on the left had long ago evaporated into a parking lot, its pop art remains, the small-roomed skeletal scars and rabid colors testifying former colorless existence, hieroglyphed on Levenspiel's brick wall; and there was a rumor around that the skinny house on the right, ten thin stories from the 1880's (Mark Twain lived there?) with a wrought-iron-banistered stoop and abandoned Italian cellar restaurant, was touched for next. Beyond that an old red-brick public school, three stories high, vintage of

1903, the curled numerals set like a cameo high on the window-smashed façade, also marked for disappearance. In New York who needs an atom bomb? If you walked away from a place they tore it down.

O

In the grimy vestibule Harry obsessively paused at the mailboxes, several maimed, hammered in, some torn out; he set down his grocery bag, his right eye twitching in anticipation of a letter from a publisher he couldn't possibly get until he had completed and sent out his long-suffering manuscript. Reverie: "We have read your new novel and consider it a work of unusual merit. We are honored to publish it." Praise for the book, not for holding out.

Lesser had held out, thirty-six, unmarried yet, a professional writer. The idea is to stay a writer. At twenty-four and twenty-seven I published my first and second novels, the first good, the next bad, the good a critical success that couldn't outsell its small advance, the bad by good fortune bought by the movies and kept me modestly at work—enough to live on. Not very much is enough if you've got your mind on finishing a book. My deepest desire is to make my third my best. I want to be thought of as a going concern, not a freak who had published a good first novel and shot his wad.

He fished an envelope out of the slot of his mailbox

with both pinkies. If he didn't some curious passer-by would. Lesser knew the handwriting, therefore source and contents: Irving Levenspiel, BBA, CCNY, class of '41, an unfortunate man in form and substance. One supplicatory sentence on thin paper: "Lesser, take a minute to consider reality and so please have mercy." With a nervous laugh the writer tore up the letter. Those he kept were from the rare women who appeared in his life, spring flowers gone in summer; and those from his literary agent, a gray-haired gent who almost never wrote any more. What was there to write about? Nine and a half years on one book is long enough to be forgotten. Once in a while a quasi-humorous inquiry, beginning: "Are you there?", the last three years ago.

I don't know where's there but here I am writing.

○

He ran with his milk, bread, fruit, up six flights, chewing a cold apple. The small green automatic elevator, built for four, had expired not long ago. The attorney at the rent office had said the landlord must keep up essential services till Lesser moved out or they would order a reduction of his rent, but since he was screwing Levenspiel by staying on, keeping him from tearing down his building, out of mercy Lesser did not complain. So much for mercy. Anyway, climbing stairs was good exercise for somebody who rarely took any. Kept a slim man in shape.

The stairs stank a mixed stench, dirt, the dirtiest, urine, vomit, emptiness. He raced up six shadowy flights, lit where he had replaced dead or dying bulbs, they died like flies; and on his floor, breathing short, pushed open the noisy fire door, into a dim, gray-walled, plaster-patched—holes with slaths showing— old-fashioned broad hallway. There were six flats on the floor, three on each side, deserted except for Les-ser's habitat on the left as one came into the hall; like turkey carcasses after a festive Thanksgiving, the knobs and locks even, picked off most of the doors by uninvited guests: bums, wet-pants drunks, faceless junkies—strangers in to escape the cold, the snow, and climbed this high up because the sixth floor lies above the fifth. Poor man's Everest, even the maimed aspire, a zoo of homeless selves. Seeking? Not glory but a bed-less bed for the small weak hours; who in the morning smashed in a window or two in payment for the night's unrepose—thereafter the wind and rain roamed the unrented flat until somebody boarded the broken glass —ransacking what they could: light fixtures, loose nails, mirrors, closet doors lifted off hinges or left leaning on one; and pissed and shat on the floor in-stead of the toilet, where it was available. Even some of the bowls were gone, or where unsnatched, their seats removed; for what purpose—hats? firewood?

pop art pieces?—in contempt of man's fate? And in the morning stumbled out, escaped into the street before this one or that was by chance unearthed by Levenspiel, up for a long-nosed snoop or pleading visit to his uncooperative writer-tenant, and threatened severely with arrest for unlawful entry and trespass. They disappeared. A smell remains.

On the roof was once an attractive small garden where the writer liked to sit after a day's work, breathing, he hoped, as he watched the soiled sky—the moving clouds, and thought of Wm. Wordsworth. Occasionally a patch of blue escaped from somewhere. Gone garden, all gone, disassembled, kidnapped, stolen —the potted flowering plants, window boxes of pansies and geraniums, wicker chairs, even the white six-inch picket fence a civilized tenant had imaginatively put up for those like him who enjoyed a moment's repose this high up in the country. Mr. Holzheimer, a German-born gentleman, originally from Karlsruhe, among those requested to move in the recent past, his six-room apartment next door to Lesser's three, desecrated now, the bedroom walls defaced, torn by graffiti, bespattered with beer, wine, varnish, nameless stains, blots, a crayon cartoon of A. Hitler wearing two sets of sexual organs, malefemale; in a second bedroom a jungle sprouted—huge mysterious trees, white-trunked rising from thick folds, crowding four walls and into the third bedroom, dense ferny underbrush, grasses sharp as razor blades, giant hairy thistles, dwarf palms with saw-toothed rotting leaves, dry thick-corded vines entangling thorny gigantic cactus exuding pus; eye-blinding orchidaceous flowers—plum, red, gold—eating alive a bewildered goat as a gorilla with hand-held penis erectus, and two interested snakes, look on. Deadly jungle. And he, Herr Holzheimer, so gentle, clean, orderly a man. I hope he comes back to haunt the bastards, for a change clean whammying unclean. Lesser tried to scare off the nightcrawlers on his floor—God knows what masked balls go on below—by playing loud his hi-fi at night; and he left every light burning when he went out of an evening. He felt, when he thought of it, a fear of the booming emptiness of the building where whole families had lived and vanished, and strangers came not to stay, but to not stay, a sad fate for an old house.

○

A sense of desolation numbed him—something lost in the past—the past?—as he entered his apartment, stoutly protected by two patent locks plus a strong snap-lock enclosing heavy circular bolts. Only when inside his safe-and-sane three rooms Lesser felt himself close off the world and relax. Here is where he forgot all he had to forget to work. He forgot amid books

packed thick along living room walls of pine shelves
he had laboriously built and varnished years ago,
mss. of two published novels and one in progress nearing its end, stored in a large carton in the closet; hi-fi
equipment, records in stacks and holders on bottom
bookcase shelves, other necessary stuff elsewhere in
closets, bureau drawers, and medicine chest. His bed-
room-study was a large uncluttered room: daybed, narrow dresser, old armchair at the window, floor lamp,
short desk plus straight-back chair—all this the evi-
dence and order of life in use. He would not think how
much of life he made no attempt to use. That was outside and he was in.

Harry, in his small kitchen, refrigerated the milk
container and considered a bit of breakfast but gagged
at the thought. He had never been one for more than
a cup of coffee; had got bread, fruit for later. Really
to give himself time to think how the writing might
go. The irresistible thing—the thought he wasn't yet
at work gave him the shakes—was to get at once to his
desk, anchor, gyroscope, magic mt.: it sits there but
moves. Long voyage in a small room. There's a long-
time book to finish. Coffee he could cook up when he
had a pageful of words on paper. You can't eat language but it eases thirst.

He entered his three-windowed study, raised the
cracked green shades without looking into the street

and arranged himself at his desk. From the top drawer he removed a portion of manuscript. Harry felt a momentary sense of loss, regret at having given his life to writing, followed by a surge of affection for the imaginative self as he read yesterday's page and a half and found it solid, sound, going well. The book redeemed him. Another two or three months ought to finish it. Then a quick last rewrite of the enterprise—call it third-and-a-quarter draft—in about three months, possibly four, and he'd have it made, novel accomplished. Triumph after just ten years. The weight of a decade lay on his head but neither cracked nor crushed—the poor head. Harry felt an impulse to inspect his face in the bathroom mirror, tired gray eyes, often bloodshot, utilitarian lips, wry, thinning, he thought, as the years went by, interested nose, observer too; but successfully resisted. A face is a face: it changes as it faces. The words he writes on paper change it. He was no longer the young man, twenty-seven, who had started this book, nor had any desire to be. Time past is time earned unless the book was badly conceived, constructed, an unknown lemon; then it's dead time. Perish the thought.

Lesser, as he wrote, was sometimes a thundering locomotive, all cars attached except caboose, cracking along the clicking tracks into a country whose topography he suspected but did not know till he got there. Lesser explorer. Lesser and Clark overland to Manifest

Destiny. Or maybe Mississippi steamboat with booming, splashing paddlewheel, heartrending foghorn, and
other marvelous inventions. Not a bad metaphor, boat.
Lesser in short-masted bark with a puff of wind in its
sail on the Galilean Lake, trying to spy out on the
apostolic shore what it's all about. Lesser sculling on
the Hudson, seeking Hendrik, listening to the booming
bowls in the metaphysical hills; or rowing to music
on the sweet-flowing Thames: he loved the moving
English water. Better still, the artist as broad swirling
river, flowing freely amid islands of experience, some
dense green, luxuriant, treeful; others barren, soft
sand with wet footprints; the flow embracing multi-
farious isles and islets, in flood tide spreading over
each and all beyond both muddy riverbanks of life and
death.

"Whereof my bowels shall sound like a harp"—
Isaiah.

Without looking up at the windows at his side the
writer imagined the wintry day beyond, crystal bright,
lit cold beauty; glad of its existence but without desire
to be in or of it, breathe its stinging glow into his half-
retired lungs, live it. This sort of pull and push he had
long ago quelled in the self else he would never have
seriously written. He itched with desire, as he wrote,
to open the nearby closet and stare at his box of ac-
cumulated manuscripts. He also half masted an erec-
tion—creativity going on. Harry scribbled with a

growing sense of pleasure as the words flowed fruit-
fully down the page. Already he tasted the satisfaction
of a good morning's work done. In the afternoon he
would type what he now wrote with his fountain pen in
longhand. Who was it who had said he thought with
his right hand? After work he would make his bed,
shower warm and cold—hot was out of the question,
and afterwards listen to some of his records with a
drink in his paw. Tonight an unexpected party, possibly a lay with a little luck; with more a bit of human
love in a mad world. You got to use words but you
got to use more than words. Lesser knew the doorbell
was ringing and went on writing. It rang insistently.

It rings forever.

○

Levenspiel ringing.

The writer sits at his desk and talks through two
rooms. He knows the words and music, they've sung
it together many times before, begun with assertions
of mutual regard. Each proclaims consideration of the
other. Lesser promises to get out as soon as he can so
the landlord can knock over his building. Levenspiel,
a thick-chested man whose voice lives in his belly,
swears he wants the other to write the best book he
can; he respects serious writers.

Goatskin siren, stop piping to my heart.

Then to business: The landlord is just back from a funeral of a close relative in Queens and thought he'd stop by to say hello. Have a little mercy, Lesser, move out so I can break up this rotten house that weighs like a hunch on my back.

Lesser argues he can't leave in the middle of a book. If he did, in his present state of mind it would take him six months to overcome distraction and get back to work, not to mention the chill he'd have facing material he'd lost the feel of. You have no idea how it changes when you're away from it. I'm afraid what will happen if my conception shifts only a little bit. You don't know what you're asking, Mr. Levenspiel.

We'll find you a nice apartment somewhere in the neighborhood where you'll be more comfortable than in this bad-smelling place. So if you stopped writing a week or two it wouldn't be the end of the world. Suppose you got sick and had to go for a while to the hospital? You're as pale as a dead fish, Lesser. You need more action, more variety out of your poor life. I don't understand how you can stay in this lousy flat every day. Think it over and listen to reason, for your own benefit.

I'm listening. I've worked hard, Levenspiel. It's my sacrifice more than yours. I'll finish soon if you have patience. My last book, for reasons I won't go into, was a bomb. I have to redeem myself in my own eyes with nothing less than a first-rate piece of work. I've practi-

cally got it done, but the last section, I confess, is re-
sisting a little. In fact it's beginning to crock me out of
my skull. Once I hit it right—it's a matter of stating
the truth in unimpeachable form, the book will be off
my chest and your back. I'll breathe easy and move
out overnight. You have my word on that, now go
away, for Jesus' sake, you're eating up writing time.

The landlord's voice grows gentler though his big
fist rhythmically pounds the locked door.

Hab rachmones, Lesser, I have my own ambition to
realize. I've got fifteen years on you, if not more, and
I'm practically naked as the day I was born. Don't be
fooled that I own a piece of property. You know already
about my sick wife and knocked-up daughter, age sixteen. Also I religiously go one afternoon every week to
see my crazy mother in Jackson Heights. All the time
I'm with her she stares at the window. Who she thinks
she sees I don't know but it's not me. She used to weigh
ninety pounds, a skinny lady, now she's two-twenty
and growing fatter. I sit there with tears. We stay together a couple of hours without words and then I
leave. My father was a worry-wart immigrant with a
terrible temper who couldn't do anything right, not to
mention make a living. He wiped his feet all over my
youth, a bastard, thank God he's dead. What's more,
everybody—*everybody*—wants financial assistance.
Now I have an opportunity, even with my limited
capital—I can get a Metropolitan Life loan—to set up

a modern six-story apartment building, five floors of big-room flats over a line of nice stores, and make myself a comfortable life if that's still possible in the world of today. Every other goddamn tenant has left out of here for a $400 settlement. You I offer $1,000 cash and you look at me as if I have a social disease. What's more, you bitch to the District Rent Office and tie me up in red tape with what not—with examiner trials, rehearings, and court appeals that'll take my lousy lawyer another year and a half to untangle it all. Outside of your $72 monthly rent, which doesn't a half pay for the oil I use on you, I have no income coming in from here. So if you're really a man, Lesser, a reasonable being, how can you deny me my simple request?

What about your tenement in Harlem?

I don't know where you find out such things, Lesser, maybe it's because you're a writer. That building I inherited from a crippled uncle, let him stay forever in his grave. It's a terrible trouble to me for reasons you know well of. I'm not speaking racially. All I'm saying is it loses me money under the present conditions. If this keeps up I'll have to abandon it. It's a disgusting state of affairs nowadays. Rent control, if you aren't afraid to listen to the truth, is an immoral situation. The innocent landlord gets shafted. What it amounts to is you're taking my legal property away from me against the Constitution.

You have an easy out, Levenspiel. Add to your projected plans for the new house you intend to build twenty percent more apartments than you're tearing down, and according to the regulations you can give me an immediate boot into the street.

A long sigh inducing heavy breathing.

I can't afford that, Lesser. It means another whole floor and possibly two. You have no idea what building costs are nowadays, twice what you estimate, and till you got the house standing, three times what you figured. I admit I had that idea before, but Novikov, my high-rise partner died, and when I thought about another partner, or to try to borrow more cash, I thought no, I will build it according to my dream. I know the kind of place I want. It's got to be comfortable to my nature. I want a smaller type house. Also I'd rather deal with five-six storekeepers than twenty-percent more tenants. It's not my nature to go after people for rent. I'm more sensitive than you give me credit, Lesser. If you were a less egotistical type you would realize it, believe me.

Lesser searches his mind. I'll tell you what I'm willing to do that might be helpful. I'll sweep the halls and stairs of the building once a week. Just leave me the janitor's broom. I don't write on Sundays.

Why not, if you're so anxious to finish your book so you can't even take off a day to move?

An old habit, the spirit rebels.

What do I care about the feshtinkineh halls here? All I want is to be able to pull this sonofabitchy building down.

The writer speaks from the depths of his being:

"It's just this last section I have left, Levenspiel. I've been working on it the better part of a year and it's still not right. Something essential is missing that it takes time to find. But I'm closing in—I can feel it in my blood. I'm proceeding within a mystery to its revelation. By that I mean whatever is bothering me is on the verge of consciousness. Mine and the book's. Form sometimes offers so many possibilities it takes a while before you can determine which it's insisting on. If I don't write this novel exactly as I should—if, God forbid, I were to force or fake it, then it's a dud after nine and a half long years of labor and so am I. After that folly what good can I expect from myself? What would I see when I look in the mirror but some deformed fourassed worm? And what's my future after that with the last of my movie money gone?—redemption in another book I'll maybe finish when I'm forty-six and starving to death?"

"What's a make-believe novel, Lesser, against all my woes and miseries that I have explained to you?"

"This isn't just any novel we're talking about. It has the potential of being a minor masterpiece. It exemplifies my best ideas as an artist as well as what life

has gradually taught me. When you read it, Levenspiel, even you will love me. It will help you understand and endure your life as the writing of it has
helped me sustain mine."

"For Christ's sake, what are you writing, the Holy
Bible?"

"Who can say? Who really knows? But not while
you're making that fucking racket. How can I think
if my mind hurts already from the sound of your
voice? My pen is dead in its tracks. Why don't you go
somewhere and let me work in peace?"

"Art my ass, in this world it's heart that counts.
Wait, you'll get yours one of these days, Lesser. Mark
my words."

His booming fist echoes in the hall.

○

Lesser had given up writing and gone to read in the
toilet. After the noise had departed he once more urged
forth the pen, but it no longer flowed though he filled
it twice. He willed but could not effect. The locomotive,
coated with ice, stood like a petrified mastodon on the
steel-frozen tracks. The steamboat had sprung a leak
and slowly sank until clamped on all sides by the Mississippi thickened into green ice full of dead catfish
staring in various directions.

Though agonized, best pretend you have stopped writing of your own accord. The day's work is done; you are relaxing in the can. It says in this book, "I should not think of devoting less than twenty years to an Epic Poem"—Coleridge. Lesser shuts his eyes and reads through the last pages of his ms. He tests his fate: He lives to write, writes to live.

○

The writer stands on the roof in the midst of winter. Around Manhattan flows a stream of white water. Maybe it is snowing. A tug hoots on the East River. Levenspiel, resembling mysterious stranger if not heart of darkness, starts this tiny fire in a pile of wood shavings in the cellar. Up goes the place in roaring flames. The furnace explodes not once but twice, celebrating both generations of its existence. The building shudders but Harry, at his desk and writing well, figures it's construction in the neighborhood and carries on as the whining fire and boiling shadows rush up the smelly stairs. Within the walls lit cockroaches fly up, each minutely screaming. Nobody says no, so the fire surges its inevitable way upwards and with a convulsive roar flings open Lesser's door.

END OF NOVEL

A WET DOG WITH A BLEEDING EYE hopped up six flights the next morning, and clawed and yelped at Lesser's door. Although it made piteous noises, Harry grabbed the mutt, alternately whimpering and snarling, by a frayed rope collar around the neck, and by offering a bony bit of stale bread every so often, succeeded in enticing him down the stairs and out of the house. It should be so easy with Levenspiel.

As he trudged up the stairs, Lesser heard muted cries, distant wailing—was there a funeral parlor on the premises? He had heard sounds of the sort before, unspecific, floating. Hard to say where or what—seemed to unpeel from city noise—unearthed?—and sing in a strange tongue. That's if you owned a certain kind of ear, not always a blessing. Hunting a real enough source of whatever it was he heard, Lesser stopped at the fifth floor and listened in the hall, his ear pressed against a knobless apartment door for telltale interior noises, possibly crowbar wrenching at a screaming wall? the landlord sneaking in a secret blow? Not bloody likely so long as the last legal tenant hadn't been formally notified—you couldn't tear down a fifth floor without displacing a sixth, even if it managed to stay afloat a while; still a palpable fear. He feared for the house and what was worse sometimes feared the house. The flat, as Lesser listened, resounded of mournful winds, Aeolus' bag. Why do wailing winds, nothing human, give off human sounds? He pushed the door and entered listening: pure deep silence. Harry wandered from room to room, the empty former kitchen minus stolen sink, a cracked washtub remaining; the living room a rectangular circle of naked hairy men disporting themselves on three walls; both bedless bedrooms despoiled; the bathtub filthy with residues of piss. Silence flowered into primal noise, utter deep silence: graveyard music.

He felt in the house, legacy of Levenspiel's visit? stronger than ever before, a presence other than himself. Nothing new but who now? Private Eye snooping for one cause or another?—you never know all the regulations of eviction. Anonymous caller drifting up from floor to foor without plan or purpose except a concealed dagger? Home is where, if you get there, you won't be murdered; if you are it isn't home. The world is full of invisible people stalking people they don't know. More homeless strangers around than ever before. God since the dawn of man should have made it his business to call out names: Jacob meet Ishmael. "I am not my brother's brother." Who says? Back in his study he wrote hurriedly, as though he had heard the end of the world falling in the pit of time and hoped to get his last word written before then.

○

One early morning when the writer, with his paper bag of bread and milk, was letting himself into his triple-locked door, he could have sworn he heard the sound of typing coming from one of the flats fronting the hall, and for an odd minute played with the thought he had left himself hard at work somewhere around while he was out getting his groceries. Lesser turned, facing the dimly lit hall.

The empty hall was empty.

Straining, he listened, and though he listened not to hear, heard the dulled clack of surely a typewriter. He felt, despite his familiarity with the sound, as though he were hearing it for the first time in his life, sensation not unmixed with competitive envy. He had been too long on one book—here was somebody writing another? Lesser felt a loss of body heat and was about to be prickly necked but gave it an after-thought: typing was typing, a typewriter, at least when in use, no lethal weapon. Still came the discomforting after-afterthought: who was the unknown typist?

Entering his flat, Harry stowed away his groceries and returned to listen in the hall. He walked stealthily past one shut door and one missing. He dipped his head into the dark open room. Nothing he could truly hear. Scouting the other side of the hall, he paused longer before each door to the end of the floor, tightly attentive to whence the continuous clicking. Again crossing the hall he located it finally next door to his, in Holzheimer's flat, astonished to have wandered far to find it close.

He was wishing Holzheimer were here to keep him company in this unpeopled place. Of course the old man was gone; and besides he couldn't type. The door was ajar. Lesser, head bent, listened. Plak plak plakity plak. Had Levenspiel set up a spy office here, CIA sub-headquarters for tuning in on Harry Lesser engaged in writing a subversive novel? Every letter he typed on paper, neatly bugged, flashed on a screen in the Attorney General's office, Department of Justice, Washington, D.C.? To end the suspense he gave the open door an adventurous thrust and it squeakily swung in. He was set to run but nobody emerged; he had to enter.

In Holzheimer's former kitchen, facing the wintry windows, sat a black man at a wooden kitchen table, typing, his back to Lesser. Though the room was perceptibly cold—the radiators and steam pipes removed, pipe openings sealed to prevent flooding, he wore over- alls cross-strapped over a green hand-knit sweater rubbed through at the white-shirted elbows. The black seemed at first a large man, but it turned out that his typewriter was large, and he, though broad-shouldered, heavy-armed, and strongly built, was of medium height. His head was bent over an old L. C. Smith, vintage of pre-World War I, resembling a miniature fortress.

The man, head bowed in concentration, oblivious of Lesser, typed energetically with two thick fingers. Harry, though impatient to be at his work, waited, ex- periencing at least two emotions: embarrassment for intruding; anger at the black intruder. What does he think he's doing in this house? Why has he come?— where from?—and how will I get rid of him? Who's got the time? He thought of phoning Levenspiel, but maybe he had booked the act. Having waited this long for acknowledgment of his presence—it was not in him to interrupt a man writing—also for a few basic facts of information, he waited longer. The black must have known someone was standing there because the open door created a draft and once Lesser sneezed; but he did not turn to look at him or whoever. He typed in seri- ous concentration, each word slowly thought out, then hacked onto paper with piston-like jabs of his stubby, big-knuckled fingers. The room shook with his noise.

This endured for five full minutes as Lesser fumed. When the typist turned his head, a goateed man, darkly black-skinned, there seemed in his large liquid eyes poised in suspension as he stared at the writer a detachment so pure it menaced; at the same time a suggestion of fright Lesser felt reflected Lesser's. His head was large, lips moderately thick, sensuous, nose wings extended. His eyes, in concentration, swelled; but he was youthful and not bad-looking, as though he considered himself not a bad-looking man and that helped. Despite the chill he seemed to be sweating.

"Man," he complained, "can't you see me writing on my book?"

Harry apologetically admitted he had. "I'm a writer myself."

That brought forth neither lightning nor thunder, nor small degree of admiration. The black stared at Lesser as though he hadn't heard, and the writer thought he might even be a little deaf until the man reacted: breathed in relief—knew now he wasn't dealing with the landlord? Had been bluffing? A smile seemed possible but did not come to pass.

On the table at the black writer's left lay a pile of well-worn, somewhat soiled, manuscript from which it seemed to Harry an unpleasant odor rose. He noticed then the man had his orange work shoes off and was sitting there writing in white wool tennis socks. Even now he wiggled his toes. Hard to say whether the sulphurous smell came from the manuscript or the feet on the floor. Maybe it's me, Lesser thought, smell of fear? Anyway, something malodorous.

Then to make his point, the point of it all—the reason he had waited to speak to the black and give notice —Lesser said, "I live here alone in this building, alone on the floor. I'm trying to finish a book."

The stranger responded to the news, rolling his eyes in thought.

"Baby, it's a hard and lonely life." His voice was low, resonant, raspy. As though relating a decision decisively arrived at, he then remarked, "I'll be working around here daily as of now on and according to the way circumstances go."

"You mean Levenspiel's letting you?" Lesser felt on the verge of frantic. He saw in the man's presence on the floor a serious threat, perhaps latest variation of the landlord's tactics of harassment.

"Which cat is that?"

"The owner of these premises, hard-luck guy. Haven't you met him—I mean wasn't it his suggestion that you work here?"

The black casually denied it. "I got no interest in any Jew landlord. Just come on this place while hunting around and entered quickly. I found this table in the cellar and the chair in a room down under here, but the light is better up high so I moved them up. I been looking for a private place to do my writing."

"What sort of writing if you don't mind me asking?"

"Now that's a personal question and what I am writing is my own business."

"Of course. All I meant, out of curiosity, was are you writing fiction or something else?"

"It might be fiction but ain't nonetheless real."

"Nobody said it wasn't."

The black said his chick was an Off-Broadway actress. "Mornings when she ain't out working, which is whenever she ain't rehearsing, the apartment's too tight for the both of us. She hangs around mixing up in my thoughts and I can't get my ass to my work. I'm not saying I don't appreciate her company, especially when my meat's frying, but not when I have something I got to write."

Lesser nodded; he knew the story.

He told the stranger Levenspiel had been trying to force him out so he could wreck the building.

"But I'm rent-controlled so he's stuck with me for a while. Harry Lesser's my name."

"Willie Spearmint."

No handshake though Harry was willing, in fact had stuck out his white paw. There it remained—extended. He was, in embarrassment, tempted to play for comedy: Charlie Chaplin, with his moth-eaten mustache, examining his sensitive mitt to see if it was a hand and not a fish held forth in greeting before he told it to come back home; but in the end Lesser withdrew it, no criticism of anyone intended or implied. Who said anybody had to shake somebody else's hand? That wasn't in the Fourteenth Amendment. He was tempted then to explain that he had, as a boy, for years lived at the edge of a teeming black neighborhood in South Chicago, had had a friend there; but in the end skipped it. Who cares?

Lesser felt ashamed he had bothered Willie Spearmint. If a man typed—a civilized act—let him type where he would. Mind your business.

"Sorry I interrupted you. Better be getting back to my own work now—on my third novel."

No response from Willie other than the absent-minded descent of a nod.

"It was a surprise to find somebody else up here typing away. I had got used to being the only man on the island."

Though tempted not to—he bit his tongue for time was of the essence, he was late getting to work—Lesser heard himself say, "Well, pardon again, I hate interruptions myself. Still, knock on my door if you have to, should you need something—eraser, pencil, whatever. I'm in the flat on your left and generally free in the late afternoon after the day's work, the later the better."

Willie Spearmint, obviously a dedicated man, stretched both green-sleeved arms aloft, wiggling his stubby fingers with ease and contentment so that

Lesser envied him, then bent over the large black machine and, focusing on the words, went on plakity plak as before. If Lesser was still present he didn't seem to know it.

○

Harry reflected in his study how much he had liked, all things considered, being alone on the top floor. I think of myself as a lonely guy, which is to say I am the right man for the work I do, which is to say, in these circumstances. I may hate going up six dark flights wondering who am I going to meet next, man or beast—but otherwise I've enjoyed this big empty house. Lots of room for the imagination to run around in. Fine place to work when Levenspiel is somewhere collecting his rents, or otherwise keeping busy. The truth of it is I could do without Willie Spearmint.

○

Shortly after noon—after a nearby siren yelped for a few seconds to remind one, if he had forgotten, of the perilous state of the world—Willie kicked on Lesser's door with the heel of his shoe, holding in both arms, in fact weighed down by it, his massive typewriter. Lesser, for a surprised second, couldn't imagine why he had come, was startled by the sight of him. Willie wore a blue-and-purple sack-like woolen African tunic over his overalls. His hair wasn't Afro-styled, as Lesser had thought, but combed straight as though against the grain, with a part on the left side, and raised in back like a floor plank that had sprung up. The stringy goatee flowering under his chin lengthened his face and seemed to emphasize the protrusive quality of his eyes, more white than brown. Standing, he was about five ten, taller than Lesser had imagined.

"Could I park this gadget here till the morning? I would hate to have it stolen out of my office. I been hiding it in the closet but that ain't hiding, if you dig."

Lesser, after hesitation, dug. "Are you through for the day?"

"What's it to you?"

"Nothing, I only thought—"

"I go on from eight to twelve or thereabouts," said the black, "full four hours' work and then goof off— visit friends and such. Writing down words is like hitting paper with a one-ton hammer. How long do you stay on it?"

Lesser told him about six hours a day, sometimes more.

Willie uneasily said nothing.

Harry asked about his manuscript. "Wouldn't you like to leave that too? Needless to say I'd respect its privacy."

"No siree, man. That stays with papa. I have my briefcase for that."

A bulky zippered briefcase was squeezed under his left arm.

Lesser understood how he felt. The safety of your manuscript was a constant worry. He kept a copy of his in a metal box in a nearby bank.

"About what time will you be coming for the machine?"

"Make it like eight or around that if it's no skin off you. If I miss a day don't fret on it."

This man's making me a daily chore. But on consideration Lesser said, "I'm up then except on Sundays."

"Sundays I ball my sweet bitch."

"Well, I envy you that."

"No need to, man, there's meat all around."

"The women I meet generally want to get married."

"Stay away from that type," advised Willie.

He lugged his typewriter into Lesser's flat and after surveying the living room laid it with a grunt under a small round table near the window, with a potted geranium in a saucer on it.

"It'll be handy here."

The writer offered no objection.

"Man, oh man." Willie gazed around in envious pleasure at the shelves crammed with books, books on their backs, magazines, some small objects of art. He inspected Lesser's hi-fi, then slowly shuffled through a stack of records, reading aloud titles and artists, mocking some of the names he couldn't pronounce. A Bessie Smith surprised him.

"What's this girl to you?"

"She's real, she talks to me."

"Talking ain't telling."

Lesser wouldn't argue.

"Are you an expert of black experience?" Willie slyly asked.

"I am an expert of writing."

"I. hate all that shit when whites tell you about black."

Willie roamed into Lesser's study. He sat at his desk, fingered his typewriter, tested the daybed mattress, opened the closet, peered in, shut the door. He stood at the wall examining some small prints the writer had collected.

Lesser explained about his movie money. "I made forty thousand dollars on a film sale about eight years ago and took it all in deferred payments. Less my agent's commission and living on roughly four thousand a year, I've done fine until now."

"Man, if I had that amount of bread I'd be king of Shit Mountain. What are you going to do after it's gone?"

"It's almost gone. But I expect to finish my book by

summer, or maybe before if my luck holds out. The advance on it should carry me into the next book another two or three years. That'll be a shorter one than this."

"Takes you that long, I mean like three years?"

"Longer, I'm a slow writer."

"Raise up your speed."

Willie took a last look around. "This is a roomy pad. Why don't we party here some night real soon? Not this week but maybe next. I'm full up this."

Lesser was willing. Though he didn't say so, he hoped Willie would bring along a lady friend or two. He had never slept with a black girl.

○

Willie Spearmint usually knocked on Harry Lesser's door at a quarter to eight. The end-of-year weather was bad and now, as he wrote, the black kept his orange shoes on and wore a thick blood-red woolen hat against the cold. He pulled it down over his ears and kept his tunic on. Harry offered to have an old heater fixed he would then lend to him, but Willie said that once he got going with the writing it warmed him to his toes.

Not so Lesser. Some days he typed with a scarf around his neck and his overcoat spread on his knees. His feet froze even with the heater going.

If it had been sleeting or heavily snowing, Willie's goatee, when he appeared at the door in the early morning, was laced with ice or snow. He beat his wet hat against Lesser's door to knock off the slush. Sometimes he looked unsettled, sullen to a degree the weather couldn't account for. And except for picking up his machine and returning it at noon, he had little to say to Harry and requested not even a glass of water during the day although the faucets had been removed and sealed off in Holzheimer's kitchen. Fortunately the toilet in Mr. Agnello's flat diagonally across the hall flushed once in a while so he relieved himself there when he had to.

One drizzly morning, Harry, stuck for a transition between scenes, was standing at the window trying to draw up an idea out of the street, the city, the human race, when he saw Levenspiel drive up in front of the pockmarked gray house across the street and park his Oldsmobile at the curb. The landlord gazed up at the window just as the writer was drawing down the shade. Lesser went at once to Willie's place and knocked on the door. No response, so he turned the knob and, calling out his own name, entered.

Willie was sucking the point of a yellow pencil stub over a difficult spot in his manuscript. He gazed at Lesser in anger at the interruption.

Lesser said the landlord was on his way up.

The black glared at him in haughty coldness.

"Fuck his ass."

"Fine," Lesser said uncomfortably, "but I thought I'd let you know." He apologized for barging in. "I wasn't sure you'd heard my knock."

Willie's expression as he contemplated the page he was working on slowly altered. He seemed uncertain, concerned if not worried.

"How will that dude know I'm here if I sit still and don't move the air? He don't go around peeking in every apartment, does he?"

Lesser didn't think so. "Usually he comes up to nudgy me while I'm writing, but he might just walk into your place when you weren't expecting it. That's his type. My advice is you ought to duck down to the floor below and wait till he's gone. Take your manuscript with you and I'll hide the typewriter. I'll let you know the minute he leaves."

They quickly carried out the operation, Willie going down to the fifth floor with his briefcase, hastily stuffed, and Lesser hid the L. C. Smith in his bathtub. Not that Levenspiel would get his intrusive foot in the door, but one never knew. Every six months, just to be a nuisance, he insisted on his prerogative to inspect the flat.

The landlord several minutes later pressed Lesser's bell, then knocked sternly on the door. The writer pictured him coming up the stairs, breathing noisily, holding the banister all the way. Levenspiel rolled a little as he walked. Better he saved himself the long trek; he looked like a heart attack type.

"Open up a minute, why the hell don't you?" Levenspiel called, "so I can talk to you man to man."

"I'm hard at work," Lesser answered from the living room, scanning a newspaper as he waited for the landlord to go. "Nothing new to report. The writing moves, there's progress."

A moment of listening silence. When he spoke, Levenspiel's rumble was throaty, low, closer to the self, as though he had gone for a walk in the park, thought things over, and was trying for better effect.

"You remember," he said, "I told you about my daughter, Lesser?"

Lesser remembered. "The knocked-up girl?"

"That's right. So she took her pennies out of the savings account that she started at age six and bought herself an abortion according to the new law. God knows what kind of a doctor she got, I've heard stories. Anyway, she didn't consult me for advice. The upshot was they penetrated the uterus with a curette and a hemorrhage started. My wife is frantic about blood poisoning. I'm on my way to the hospital to see my baby in intensive care."

"I'm sorry, Levenspiel."

"I just thought I'd tell you. You can't tell everybody

such things, but I thought maybe to a writer."

"Accept my sympathy."

"I accept," said the landlord, "so much as you can spare."

"So what else is new?" he said after an unused minute.

"Nothing."

"Nothing at all?"

"Nothing."

"No change in your attitude to the human race?"

"It still salutes."

Levenspiel left in silence.

Lesser tried to wrestle the incident out of his mind. Clever bastard, he knows I feel guilt. Another dollop on my head and I'll go through the floor down to the cellar. That's his plan, I bet.

Willie, watching from a window below, had seen the landlord leave the house and had hastened up. He tapped on Lesser's door and lifted the typewriter out of the tub.

"Fartn Jew slumlord."

"Willie," said Lesser, "if it's news to you I'm Jewish myself."

"All I'm saying is an economic fact."

"I'm telling you a personal one."

"Thanks anyway for swinging with me, baby. Lots of appreciation."

"My pleasure."

The black smiled, beautiful teeth, a rare gesture.

"Let's have that party we were planning on, this Friday night. I'll bring my bitch and tell a few friends."

○

Willie's friends who climbed up the six frozen flights to Lesser's flat during a blizzard on the first Friday of the new year, a dusting of snow on their heads, included his "bitch," Irene Bell, to Lesser's somewhat surprise—that she was Willie's taste, he had expected a less striking type—a white girl verging on beautiful. She hadn't quite made it; he couldn't guess why, as though beauty were more of an obligation than she cared to assume. She had glanced at Lesser's small mirror on the wall—her eyes wavered—and turned away in annoyance as she removed her voluminous cape. She wore on her face a depleted smile, sour at the edges, and troubled eyes. Some sadness. Lesser stared at her. Willie, when he got around to introducing her to him, said she was his white chick, not giving her name. At that she walked away. The writer figured they had quarreled on their way over.

The other two people were a black couple: Mary Kettlesmith, a hardassed attractive girl with an animated open face and fine figure. She wore a natural of small silken ringlets, and a plain white mini with purple tights. She talked easily, touching Lesser's arm with ten fingers when Willie introduced them. He touched hers and felt various hungers. Sam Clemence, her eyeglassed Afro'd boyfriend, was a quiet type on his way to stoned. Harry had not much impression of him one way or another. He himself was not in rare shape. He had expected fourteen people but because of the weather there were only five; he felt forlorn, a fool for not having invited a woman for himself.

Willie, as though unable to bear parting with it, wore his writing sweater, decorated with a string of Arabian glass beads as large as walnuts. Otherwise he was dolled up in hip-hugging yellow pants and two-tone brown-and-black shoes, wet from the snow. His goatee and hair had been combed and creamed, and he seemed to be engaged in enjoying himself. He moved lightly, strutting, finger-popping. Though he pretended no great wit, what he said made them laugh and his gestures were witty. Now and then he glanced at Irene sitting by the window, sometimes blankly, as if trying to remember something he had forgotten. Or heard voices? Here was something new of the stranger levitated out of the street up to the floor where Lesser for months had lived alone, housemate now, fellow writer, maybe future friend. His lonely girl, possibly waiting for a good word, looked on from a detached distance. If Willie noticed he seemed not much affected; he kidded with those close by. Lesser thought how easily he shucks off the writing self, whereas he, in his active mind, rarely stopped writing. He determined tonight to take pleasure.

Though pretending not to, Lesser looked Willie's Off-Broadway actress over carefully. He pretended, not she; Irene sat as though to say she was no more than he saw, had no statement to make about herself. She was about twenty-five, her long dyed blond hair drawn thickly over her left shoulder, where it lay across her bosom like an emblem—the mystery why it all but wounded the host. Two women walk into my house and in a minute flat I'm standing on my hands. He greeted an old self.

Come out of momentary seclusion and whatever mood, the actress pulled off damp boots and, drink in hand, explored the apartment, slightly pigeon-toed in large narrow feet suiting a tallish girl. Where she had been Lesser breathed in gardenia scent. He was partial to flowers. She wore a buttoned short skirt and a flushed pink blouse, her milkwhite breasts visible when she bent to rub away a cigarette ash stain on her knee. She sat on his hassock with legs parted. Lesser looked all the way up. Irene rose as though she had sat on an egg; she said something to Mary, who laughed into cupped hands.

Lesser escaped to his study.

My God, why are all my desires visible?

After a while he returned to music going on; his guests were dancing, Mary, gorgeously, with Sam; Irene with Willie; Lesser suspected she had sought him out, not vice versa. They danced to some rock records Willie had brought along in a paper bag, a boogaloo of rolling shoulders and butts. And though they danced as if in truth conjoined, Willie's mocking heavy eyes concentrating, Irene gyrating around him with muted smile set on pale face, as if the face weren't dancing, and with nobody but each other, the writer sensed they moved partly as though to hold off contact although talking intently all the time. Trying to assess degree of mutual discontent—or was he kidding himself, was this apparent resistance to the other a mode of attachment, an emotion ambivalently stronger than pure anything else? Lesser twice attempted to slip in between them but neither of the dancers would have it. Yet at one point Irene slapped Willie; he slapped her harder; she wept for a minute and they went on dancing.

Lesser cut in on Sam and Mary. Sam momentarily held tight but Mary eluded him and stepped up to Harry. The black girl danced with him as though going on in a dance previously begun. Her eyes were shut, her movements sexy. Lesser stopped to watch her twist. Mary, opening her eyes, laughed, held forth both arms; he came forward doing his little thing as she shook exotically. Her steps were quick, graceful, magical; she danced the leaves to Lesser's tree. He loosened up, swung himself around, Mary encouraging him. As they boogalooed in the center of the room—Sam pissing out of a window at the blizzard— Mary whispered to Lesser that she lived no more than two blocks away. After considering the intent of her information, in his study later, he made a play for her, when the rock was loud, Sam in half a stupor, and Willie and Irene still engaged in their curious courtship ritual.

Aroused by Mary, Lesser kissed her and slipped his fingers into her brassière; she, breathing heavily, kissed wetly in return but showed not much inclination when he tried to lead her to the daybed. She seemed to weigh something in herself, then with a sigh squeezed his hands and put them away.

Her eyes bright, she stood with pelvis thrust forward, neck arched. Her breasts were small, body slender, legs slim and beautifully formed. Harry, erected, hoping his desire would inspire hers, lifted her mini over her purple tights.

Mary forcefully shoved him away. "Split, honky, you smell."

Lesser felt desire ebb out of him.

"I didn't mean to offend you."

After a tense minute she softened, then quickly

kissed him. "Now don't take on personally. I have to set my mind up for sex, that's how I am. Just be like nice and I'll be nice to you. Okay now?"

Harry offered her an artificial violet from a pitcherful on the windowsill. Mary took the flower, looked for where to pin it on her dress, then dropped it into her purse on the daybed.

He apologized once more.

"Don't hold it against yourself, Harry. I like you fine."

"Then what's this smell you mentioned?"

"Like you smell white is all I mean."

"How does white smell?"

"No smell at all."

"So I won't worry."

"Don't," she said. "Life is too short, okay now?"

Sam glared into the room, and Mary, taking her purse, went to him. Lesser warned himself not to let his poor party turn into a bad scene.

○

Harry requests to borrow a strawberry-papered joint from Willie.

Willie offers to share his. They sit crosslegs on the small kitchen floor, shoulder to shoulder, passing a rumpled wet cigarette back and forth.

This here is part Lebanon hashish. Don't smell it, boy, suck it in your gut.

Lesser holds the sweet-burning smoke down till the room turns radiant and grand. Arches soar, the rose window flushes deep rose. Bells bong in a drowned chapel.

Now this cathedral is a floating island smelling of forest and flowers after summer rain. The roots of a thousand trees trail in the yellow water. We're alone on this floating island, Willie, full of evergreens and wild purple roses. We're moving with the current. Bells toll in the deep woods. People on both shores of the river are waving as we sail by. They wave red white and black flags. We have to bow, Willie. I'm bowing on this side. They're cheering and I'm bowing. You better bow, too.

Thanks, folks, my next will be my best.

Who are those cats, brothers or ofays?

Black cats with white hats and white ones with black hats. They're hip hip hooraying because we're good writers. We confess the selves we pretend to know. We tell them who they are and why. We make them feel what they never knew they could. They cry at our tears and laugh to hear us laugh, or vice versa, it makes no difference.

What's your book about, Lesser?

Love, I guess.

Willie titters, rowing calmly, steadily, his muscles flashing as the water ripples.

It's about this guy who writes because he has never really told the truth and is dying to. What's yours about, Willie?

Me.

How's it coming?

On four feet, man, in a gallop. How's yours?

On one. Clop.

I'm gon win the fuckn Noble Prize. They gon gimme a million bucks of cash.

After me, Willie. I've worked since the ice age and tomorrow is another day.

Willie rows coolly, sighting ahead in the swift shifting current of the broadening river, watching out for snags and sandbars and the hulks of wrecked ships.

What's more I'm writing my best book. I want all the good people on both shores waving their little paper flags, all those grays and blacks, to admit Harry Lesser is King David with his six-string harp, except the notes are words and the psalms fiction. He is writing a small masterpiece though not too small. How small are the psalms?

Lesser gives three clops for Harry Lesser.

Pile it on, man. Pile on the shit. Pile on the coal and let's see the smoke. Pile on the bread. You can have the noise they makin but I gon shovel up the bread.

It's only money, Willie. What of remembrance in future time, a small immortality? Consider the human condition and how soon gone.

I want green power. I want money to stuff up my black ass and white bitch's cunt. I want to fuck her with money.

Think of this sacred cathedral we're in, Willie, with lilting bonging iron bell. I mean this flower-massed, rose-clustered, floating island. I guess what I mean is what about art?

Don't talk flippy. I worry about it gives me cramps in my motherfuckn liver. Don't say that dirty word.

Art is the glory and only a shmuck thinks otherwise.

Lesser, don't bug me with that Jewword. Don't work your roots on me. I know what you talkin about, don't think I don't. I know you tryin to steal my manhood. I don't go for that circumcise shmuck stuff. The Jews got to keep us bloods stayin weak so you can take everything for yourself. Jewgirls are the best whores and are tryin to cut the bloods down by makin us go get circumcise, and the Jewdoctors do the job because they are afraid if they don't we gon take over the whole goddamn country and wipe you out. That's what they afraid. I had a friend of mine once and he got circumcise for his Jewbitch and now he ain't no good in his sex any more, a true fag because he lost his pullin power. He is no good in a woman without his pullin power. He sit in his room afraid of his prick. None of that crap on me, Lesser, you Jew-bastard, we tired of you fuckn us over.

If you're an artist you can't be a nigger, Willie.

WILLIE

Nigger, nigger, never die
Shinin face and bulgin eye.

LESSER

Nigger, nigger, shining bright
In the forest of the night.

Willie rows until his eyes are white stones. He rows as he sleeps. The shores of the river fade in the dark. The cheers are silent stars. The floral island disappears in mist. A galaxy moves like a jeweled wheel in the night sky.

I'm gon drop a atom bomb on the next white prick I see.

Lesser wrestles clouds of mosquitoes.

○

Lesser, lonely at his sad little party, gets to talk to Willie's girl. She had been wandering through living room and study, perhaps to evade him. There was no peace in her eyes or big feet. When he had been about to cut into her dance with Willie he heard him say, "Irene, I can't lay up with you tonight. You know how hard that part I am now writing on my book has got. I need my strength and juice on my work tomorrow. Wait till Sunday."

"I hate your shitty book," Irene had said.

The heat had gone off and the apartment was cold. Irene lay under her long cape on Lesser's sofa, and when the writer tentatively got under it with her she let him, saying nothing. The gardenia scent rose from her body touched with a faint odor of sweat. Sam and Mary, Afro to Afro, were asleep in the study on the daybed with the electric heater on. Willie, a joint in his mouth, was still rowing on the kitchen floor.

Irene wore on her blond head a chaplet of wax violets she had woven from a bunch one of the women of Lesser's past had left in a small cracked pitcher on a window in his study. They were faded but brought out the bluish green of her eyes. Lesser had noticed she bit her nails to the quick, plucked her brows clean and badly smeared on brown penciled ones. One was too long, one too short. This gave her face a clownish touch. He was sure her discontent was with herself.

"What's the true color of your hair?"

"Black," she mocked, in a low voice. "And my name is Belinsky, not Bell. And Willie has been my lover for two years. What else do you want to know? I know why you're lying here. You heard him say he wouldn't sleep with me tonight. I saw you listening."

"I wouldn't mind offering my creative juice."

"Fuck off, I'm Willie's girl."

It was a bleak night. Lesser heard himself apologizing again.

"It's not because of what I heard Willie say. When you came into the house tonight I felt this sense of something I'd lost in the past."

"What past?"

"As though I hadn't been where I should've been once when you wanted someone."

"I got the one I wanted."

Lesser wondered how the writing would go in the morning. Probably badly.

"What's your book about?" Irene asked.

"Love," he said, his breath rising.

"What do you know about love?"

Lesser wouldn't say.

She fell asleep with a sour smile.

Willie appeared in the room.

"Like cool it, man," he said to Lesser on the sofa. "None of that apeshit on me."

○

When Willie and his friends left the apartment the blizzard had spent itself. The black, his eyes still glassy, slapped Lesser on the back.

"We groove on art, dad. You and I are gonna be real tight."

They embraced like brothers.

○

A few hours later when Willie came in for his typewriter he spoke not a word to Lesser though his lips worked nervously. His expression was tense. He seemed like a man staring at two thoughts, neither of which he could stand.

Lesser at first was afraid Irene had told him he had tried to make her after overhearing Willie's remark to her. Or had Mary Kettlesmith described his acrobatics with her miniskirt?

But Willie had nothing to say, and alarmed at the thought of an argument that might upset the morning he was balancing like a ball on his nose, the writer offered strict silence in return. He was more than a little hung up, stupid from lack of sleep, worried about his work.

Willie, with a grunt, lifted his machine and stepped into the hall. Lesser shut the door in relief and was immediately writing. He worked steadily into a very good day; this sometimes happened when he was worried little sleep would lock the gears of concentration. At half past twelve the black had not appeared. At seven that night, washing his two supper dishes, the writer found himself wondering if—wishing?—Willie had for some reason cut out of here, located himself a new place to work. Maybe an abandoned apartment house all to himself? Lesser could do without his daily don't-do-me-any-favors visits although he was willing to help a fellow writer out. Writers helped writers. Up to a point: *his* writing came first.

At 9 P.M., Lesser reading in his rocker, Willie kicked the door, hugging his machine as though he were pregnant with it. After setting it under the table, the black after a minute of fixed thought, said: "Lesser, I have to pull your coat about a certain matter."

The writer apologized in advance for his behavior last night.

"It was the hashish I'd say. It doesn't agree with me. I'd better stay away from the stuff."

Willie flicked his nail along the part in his hair. After a while he scratched both pink palms with hard brown nails and blew into his stubby-fingered fist. He shuffled one foot, then the other.

Lesser was uncomfortable. Has he been seeing old Stepin Fetchit films, or is something the matter with him?

Willie spoke brusquely. "I thought I would leave my manuscript of my book here tonight."

"Ah, it's welcome," Harry said, relieved if that was

all. "Don't worry about anybody reading it. You have my word on that."

Willie drew a restless heavy breath. "Man, I'm *asking* you to read it."

He bent as though afflicted by a spasm but at once straightened up.

"Like I have a belly ache about my work." Sweat gleamed on his brow. He touched dry lips with his pink tongue. It seemed to Lesser he had never seen his eyeballs so large before, inflated, white, scared.

"Belly ache?"

"On my writing. I am revising some of it again but every time I read it I do something very new, like I never got it right in the first place. The picture keeps shifting on me, you know what I mean? Yesterday I thought I laid down some good pages but when I was reflecting about them in my chick's apartment the whole scene I wrote blew up in my mind like a brick shithouse. Man, that wipes you out. I didn't feel like coming to your party. I wanted to go on back to my work and stay on it till I got the wrong stuff out and the right stuff in but Irene told me to renew myself with some relaxation and fun. Today I sat in my office all day reading on my book and I have this fuckn feeling I rode off the main track in some places but I don't exactly know where that starts or why it does. Anything I read now looks blurred up, as if I am wearing my grandpappy's eyeglasses, and throws me off my

balance. I feel like I am somewhere else than I ought to be. What do you think I have to do now, Lesser?"

The writer, conscious Willie was seriously asking for advice, answered cautiously.

"If you get the right distance it's easier to regain perspective. Sometimes I pick up an earlier chapter and retype it, at the same time making notes about the one that doesn't satisfy me. That's one way of quickening insight, there are others."

"I tried all that crap," Willie said impatiently. "Lesser," he went on, trying to restrain the emotion in his voice, "I could save on lots of worry and trouble if you could put your eye on what went wrong."

"You want me to read your manuscript?"

Willie, averting his stiffened eyes, nodded. "Nobody else I know has got two novels published."

Harry reluctantly agreed. "I will if you really want me to."

What more could a man say?

"Would I ask you if I didn't want you to?" The black threw him a look of hatred as he left the room.

○

Harry slowly read the funky manuscript of the touchy man, almost two hundred oversize thick pages. He read at first against the will, two sentences for every one. He read of two minds—curious; resistant. He had

promised Willie but after this nothing more. No further involvements with his dissatisfactions, sentiments, labor.

The wind in the street complained as he read holding a handkerchief to his nose to keep off fumes. He hadn't heard so pure and sustained a keening outside his window in the almost ten years he had lived in the house, the wind like a live ghost haunting itself. A door slammed in the distance and slammed again, Lesser jumping twice as he read. He heard whispering voices in the hall. Willie, wandering, talking to himself? Levenspiel muttering? Explorers from a ship offshore? Or the lower depths? Going to the door, he put his eye to the keyhole. Nothing he could make out but gloomy hall. Lesser unbolted the door and went in his sneakers to Willie's office, expecting momentarily to hear his smoking plak plak, though the formidable typewriter visibly sat under the table by the window as he read. Not a serious inside sound of any sort. Maybe a rat scuttled down a toilet hole. Nothing really happening but imagination working overtime, the writer's bag. You worked with it, you had to live with this hyperactive genie. Yet he listened obsessively as though he might lose some small bite of experience if he didn't; then tapped with his fingernails on the door, turned the tense knob and entered. Pure black night, no moon or stars. Who could see a black in all this black?

"Willie?" Harry whispered.

He snapped on the one-hundred-watt bulb Willie had screwed into the socket one rainy day. The bare kitchen, lit in a glare, stared from afar. Willie's table and cracked chair—lonely, distant minus the writer writing, two hunks of wood; but if one wrote on them, a dignified desk and chair, serious business going on, the fabrication of fiction.

Lesser returned to his rooms and went on reading. The manuscript literally gave forth a gassy odor. Stench of toil?—accrued Willie Spearmint sweat plus something mildewed or smelling so? Perhaps odor of decay abetted by the chemistry of very cheap green paper—pulpy sulphurous stuff, typed on, erased often with burning, rubber-stinking eraser, typed over, et cetera? Or maybe the foul blow to the nose derived from the festering lives the words created, or their vengeful human farts?

Willie's book had once been entitled *A Nigger Ain't Shit*, crossed out for *Missing Life*, by Bill Spear, ingenious pseudonym, part surname, part tribal hunting weapon, plus overtone of Shakespear, also Willie. A third title had been very lightly penciled in. Examining it closely with his better-visioned eye, Lesser made out *Black Writer*—followed by a question mark. Anyway, the manuscript, which Lesser read slowly, making notes, in the course of three nights—Willie liked to keep the pages stacked before him on his desk as he continued to work long hours on whatever he was now writing or rewriting, at least he typed—was in two main parts, apparently a Life and Work, six chapters of the first, totaling one hundred forty-eight pages, followed by fifty of short stories concerning Harlem types living their black experience, a not bad approach to an autobiography, though Willie had never called it that. He hadn't talked much about his book. Lesser had thought of it as a novel possibly because he was writing one himself.

The book, although for various reasons not a finished piece of work, was absorbing to read, Willie's human history: from "Downsouth Boy" to "Black Writer"; via progression "Upsouth," "Harlem Nights," "Prison Education." The short last chapter was entitled, "I Write for Black Freedom." The book was mainly naturalistic confessional, Willie's adventures simply narrated, the style varying from Standard English to black lingo, both the writing and psychology more sophisticated than Lesser would have guessed. "I" grows up in redneck Mississippi in pure black poverty. He is knocked around by kith and kin more than whites, but it seems to him his first major insight into his life is how much he hates *them* for maiming the blacks who maim him, in particular his miserable meager mother and white-ass-kissing stepfather. One day, Willie, age thirteen, stepping out of the path of an approaching Charlie wearing a straw boater, shuts his eyes tight so The Man won't see in them the image of Black Boy crushing under his heel the white's bloody balls. "My hate of him was so pure it warmed me the rest of my life."

To escape the primal cemetery, Eden where nothing black grows green, he hops a freight to Detroit. "Where I spend the most of my days cleaning out white shitstalls for the Ford Company." And on the side breaks into clothes lockers to steal loose cash; at which, in spite of some tight squeaks, he is never caught. He finally has to face up to the self-hatred living in him like a sick dog in a cellar. This comes like a kick to his head after he beats half to her death his black bitch for no reason he is sure of. He accuses her of sleeping with a white man though she swears, and he in his heart believes, she hadn't. What he had done to his broken-faced seventeen-year-old girl becomes terrified awareness of something frightening in his nature. The panic of his guilt causes him to split. "I thought if I looked in a mirror it would show I had turned white." But the depression that afflicts him is because he is black.

Willie grooves through the Harlem scene in skin-tight satin pants and fast buckskin shoes, from jazz to jail in easy stages, through numbers, hustling, pimping two white whores. "All you got to know is a white chick loves a black prick." He pushes hard stuff, and while sick for dope—nose running, cramps, nausea—attempts housebreaking and burglary at which he is caught by two big white pigs he fights in terror with his bare fists. "On my first solo gig I was bagged out of my own stupidity, beaten shitless, and dumped in jail." He is tried, convicted, and sent to prison for a five calendar stretch. His new discovery is "How low your misery can go. All day I walk on myself and the shit sticks to my shoes." He hurts in terrible ways. But the hurt hurts less once you begin to hear the blues deep down in you. He listens and hears. "Willie Spearmint sing this song."

Time is slow and sickening but by some crazy mix of pain, luck, and what he still has left of his will, serving time serves him. "Stopping your running you have the time to think. I think clearer about myself, who I am, and if I will ever be more than the lowest." "If they didn't put me away then I would've murdered somebody for sure." To take his mind off the soul-destroying prison, to teach himself what he had to know to survive, to put himself together better than he was, Willie begins to read in the prison library. "Once I got started on that I never stopped. I read one book after the other, slow at first, then quicker once I get to know more words." At first he read fiction more than anything else. He read some Dickens, Dreiser, James Farrell, Hemingway, Richard Wright, Ellison, Baldwin and others. "And I read hundreds of short stories from the word go right up to modern times, both black and white." "And while I am reading I have this important, exciting and also frightening playback in me *that I can write*." "It isn't hard to do when you have just finished reading one story you have liked to make it go on further. Or change the ending. Or write something like it." He wonders if he can write stories that have happened to him. "And the next thing I know my head is so crammed full of them I can't separate one from the other." Willie laughs, shouts, and dances in his cell. He begs for paper and pencil, gets them, and sits down at his table. He writes about the real funk of life. He writes in tears. "I cry for my goddamn mother, and everybody black I write about, including myself." He loves the words he puts on paper; out of them black people are born. He loves who they are, their voices and their wit. Willie gets high when he writes, this pleasure is the sweetest. As the sentences fill up the pages and the people and their actions come alive, his heart fills with pride. "From then on I am not afraid of the fucking prison because I am out of it as much as I am in. I am in my imagination. I swear to myself I will be the best writer, the best Soul Writer." He writes dozens of stories. "The more I write on the terrible and violent things of my life, the more I feel easier on myself. The only thing I am afraid of, I don't want to get too soft in my nature."

Willie also mentioned reading some of the revolutionary writers because he wanted to know more what the whole scene was about. He read in Marx, Lenin, Trotsky, Mao. He read every book he could about black men: books on Africa, slavery, black customs and culture. He kept notes in a looseleaf notebook, but when he tried to write about issues usually it came out little stories about black people. In the main he wrote fiction. As Willie came to a broader understanding of his people's history and the injustice of their suffering, he felt for them a deep, sweet, overpowering love. For the whites he kept his hatred. Maybe not in his mind every minute of the day but he kept it in principle. When he was sprung out of prison, he left with five folders full of writing he had pledged to the cause of Black Freedom.

This was the end of the autobiographical section; then came the short stories. None of Willie's protagonists fared as well as he. No one of them found a way to save himself.

Bugsy is shot thirty-eight times in Catshit Alley by two white pigs who had cornered him there after a mugging. He had shot back with his razor, flung it once.

Ellery is cooked to death in Sing Sing. He had tried to convince the judge, "Judge, you got the wrong black man. Black is an easy color to recognize if you lookin for a nigger. I swear to you out of the bottom of my heart I did not kill a white man on that dark night. I am not the one you think I am."

Daniel chokes his father to death for spitting in his mother's face. After, he asks his mama to forgive him and she says she might but the Lord won't. "I don't know why I do it, why I kill him all the way," Daniel says. "I guess I hate him more than I hate you."

In a weird story called "No Heart," this unnamed black man has a hunger to murder a white and taste a piece of his heart. It is simply a strong thirst or hunger. He tricks a drunken white down into a tenement cellar and kills him. He cuts into the dead man but can't find the heart. He cuts into his stomach, bowel, and scrotum, and is still cutting when the story ends.

In the last piece Harry (Harry?) is painted white by three brothers after they had considered stomping on him, or maybe tar and feathers, for what he did. He had betrayed a numbers runner, his friend Ephraim, to the pigs. Ephraim had taken his true bitch away from him. The runner's friends trap Harry in his room and force him to strip off his clothes. They pour three cans of white lead paint all over him as he kneels on the floor, the paint so thick on his head only his eyes are black. He escapes into the hall and runs up the roof stairs as they pursue him. The last they see of him is Harry leaping off the roof into the street below, a white nigger lighting up the night.

Five stories, five deaths—four blacks, one white. The violence shows the depth of Willie's unspent rage. Maybe his tears had scorched the paper and stunk up the pages? On rereading the book Lesser, though he sniffs now and then, smells no smell at all.

○

Lesser is moved by Willie's writing. For two reasons: the affecting subject of the work, and the final sad feeling that he has not yet mastered his craft. My God, what he's lived through. What can I say to a man who's suffered so much personal pain, so much injustice, who clearly finds in his writing his hope and salvation, who defines himself through it? He comes in the end, as in the old slave narratives, to freedom, through his sense of writing as power—it flies up and carries him with it—but mainly in his belief that he can, in writing, help his people overthrow racism and economic inequality. That his freedom will help earn theirs. The Life he writes, whatever he calls it, moves, pains, inspires, even though it's been written before, and better, by Richard Wright, Claude Brown, Malcolm X, and in his way, Eldridge Cleaver. Their self discoveries have helped Willie's. Many black men live the same appalling American adventure, but it takes a unique writer to tell it uniquely, as literature.

To make black more than color or culture, and outrage larger than protest or ideology. Willie has good ideas for stories but doesn't always build them well; in the end they fall short of effective form. Lesser sees irrelevancy, repetition, underdeveloped material; there are mistakes of arrangement and proportion, ultimately of focus. There's more to do than he does. On the other hand, he seems to be sensitive to good writing and that may account for his suspicions concerning his own. He writes with feeling, no doubt with pleasure, yet senses he ought to be dissatisfied. He may not even know that his writing shows impatience with the craft of writing. I think he wants me to point this out to him. Should I do it—say what I think, or less?—soft-pedal maybe, encourage, try to even the odds, given what he's gone through? I wouldn't want to hurt a sensitive man. Yet if I don't tell him what I think is true how can I help him improve his work?

And if Lesser suppresses truth Lesser is a fake. If he's that, how can *he* go on writing?

○

When he returned the manuscript to Willie the morning after he had finished his second reading of it, Lesser said he was ready to discuss his work whenever it suited Willie's convenience. He wanted now to get it off his chest but wouldn't press. Willie, dead-pan, except for an absent smile that grazed his lips, as though he had not heard what Lesser had said but having seen his moving lips was more or less acknowledging somebody had spoken, accepted his briefcase without a word. He didn't so much as glance at it or look at Harry. On Lesser's afterthought Willie seemed wounded, hurt before the fact?—by me? unless the writer was misreading. Maybe he had a toothache, or hemorrhoids—some personal problem? Whatever that was, his silence translated into annoyance more than wound; perhaps with himself, as though he might be regretting having asked Lesser to read his book and say what he thought might be wrong with it. But in a minute the black's lips parted, he gazed into Lesser's doubtful eyes with his own heavy eyes softened, as though forgiving him for whatever he had or hadn't done, and said sonorously, "I thank you for reading it." That's all. And left so cleanly, although hauling the iron load of typewriter and weight of his book in his arms, it seemed to Lesser as though he had willed his disappearance in a prestidigitated poof. Talented man Willie Spearmint.

That same noon, in a relaxed mood—he had somewhere got a cigar—Willie remarked, "I can't stay on to talk to you now, Lesser. My bitch is itching. We partying tonight in our place and have to buy some bottles and stuff, but I'll be around in a day or two to consummate that little mutual matter."

"Suit yourself, Willie. Whenever you say. At your convenience." Mixed in was envy for not having been invited to the party at Irene's.

He's afraid, Lesser thought. Shits green. So do I, to admit the truth. It's bad enough to criticize a man's living flesh, as whose book isn't. But with color added? It's a black life, understandably touchy stuff. Lesser dreaded a little what he had let himself in for. He had felt forewarned he would have to pay for doing Willie a favor. The nature of certain things, the weight of color.

Maybe I could make it easier all around by writing him a note? On paper there's no personal confrontation—who needs it?

As he took time to write it the next morning—it was only eleven but Willie was on his mind and he was getting little done—the black knocked, not kicked at the door.

Lesser rose, nervous but relieved, eager to dump the burden that Willie had laid like a paving block on his head.

Willie, eyes downcast—obviously he'd had trouble working, because he was already putting the typewriter away under the table—as he straightened up seemed to tighten, as though no move but the next was possible and he had no love for it. He stood staring for a while out the window. Lesser looked too. He saw nothing.

Willie kept staring, then seemed to give up, as though whatever he was looking for wasn't there, if he were looking. What was there—or what there was, was in this room. In the room, whatever he was he wasn't exactly. But after a while he was with Lesser, in his study, sitting like an ebony statue in the straight-back chair, and nobody, his presence stated, was his Pygmalion. He had sculpted himself.

○

The writer, sitting forward on his daybed, rubs dry white palms together.

"Drink?"

"Let's cut out the preliminary crap and get down to where we are at."

Lesser defensively reminds Willie he hadn't asked to read his book. "You asked me to. If you think you made a mistake and are going to be stiffassed and uptight by what I say, maybe we ought to call it off before we start? I'm obliged to you for letting me see your manuscript."

"I *am* uptight, man, because it's my nature as well as my personal privilege, but let's talk anyway, dig?"

Lesser asserts he is not out to arouse anyone's antagonism. "I've got my own nature to consider. It likes to live in peace."

"My antagonism is also my privilege and don't go giving yourself too much credit for certain circumstances, like me asking you for a favor."

"All I'm saying is if we can't have a reasonable talk, let's forget it. I've been on my book for years and finally want to get it done. For that I need peace and quiet. That's why I like it up here—no serious disturbances, I can work. Levenspiel stalks me but I can stand it. Still, I wouldn't want anybody else on my tail or in my hair, with or without cause."

"Instead of preaching all those words, Lesser, why don't you get off your white ass and say your true piece? I ain't asking you to fatmouth me, just as I am not interested in getting into any argument with you."

"I heartily agree."

Lesser considers reading the part of the letter he had composed but drops that thought and says what he feels he has to as Willie, pretending patience, calm, nothing much to worry about, interlocks stubby fingers on his green-sweatered chest, then gives up immobility and strokes his little woolly beard.

Lesser says: "To start with, there's no question you're a writer, Willie. Both parts of your book, the autobiography and the five stories are strong and moving. Whatever the writing lacks there's obviously a talent at work."

Willie laughs mildly derisively. "Oh, come on, dad, who you telling that to? It don't mean anything much when you know your book is in trouble. Come on down to the cold-shit truth of it."

Lesser says the truth of it is the book is good but could be better.

"I told you that myself," says Willie. "Didn't I say I wasn't satisfied? Now go on to what I really asked you, like *where* I steered off the track."

"I was going to say if you aren't satisfied with the writing, Willie, then I guess you have reason not to be. I would say that the form of the whole is not sufficient. There's a flawed quality, what you call blurred, that gives the shifting effect that bothers you."

"Where does it *start,* man?"

"Right from the beginning of the autobiography. Not that you don't work hard but there has to be more emphasis on technique, form, though I know it's not stylish to say that. You've got to build more carefully."

Willie rises, groaning, as though somebody would nail him to the chair if he didn't.

"I want to show you how full of crud you are, Lesser, in what you just said. First off, you dead wrong in the way you classified my work. The part you call autobiography is pure made-up fiction that I invent as I go along. Man, I am makin it up. The I guy who is narratin it ain't me. That cat is straight out of my imagination all along, pure and simple, comin and goin. Myself, I was born on 129th Street in Harlem and moved to Bedford-Stuyvesant with my mama when I was six years old, and which I ain't been south of except to swim at Coney Island. I have never been in Mississippi and would not put my foot in that shithole. I never in my whole life ate chitterlins because my mama and me couldn't stand the smell of them, and I think I would throw up if I did. I never worked in Detroit, Michigan, though my true daddy did for three years in a job cleanin toilets. But on the other hand, four of the short stories happen to be dead true. They happened to brothers I knew all my life just exactly like I tell it, and everything I say really happened and that's the only real autobiography there is and there is no other, period and end of period."

Lesser admits surprise.

"The book has the tone of autobiography, but even if it's pure fiction the point is that something's not coming off right or you wouldn't have asked me to read it."

Willie calmly and thoroughly scratches his balls.

"I'm not soundin on you, Lesser, but how can you be so whiteass sure of what you sayin if my book turns out to be two different things than you thought?"

"In any case we both agree it needs more work."

"Work," Willie mimics him, his moist eyes rolling. "I've worked my ass to the flat bone. I've worked past misery, man. This is my fourth draft, how many more do I have to do?"

His low voice rose high.

"Maybe try one more."

"Fuck you on that."

Lesser is angry with himself for having got into this hassle, having known it would end as one.

"Willie," he says irritably, "I've got to get on with my own book."

Willie's bulky body sags, ebony turned tar.

"Don't put your whammy on me, Lesser, you. Don't give me that grief. Don't hit me on my self-confidence."

Lesser asks Willie to grant him good will. "I know how you feel, I put myself in your place."

In cold and haughty anger the black replies. "No ofay motherfucker can put himself in *my* place. This is a *black* book we talkin about that you don't understand at all. White fiction ain't the same as *black*. It *can't* be."

"You can't turn black experience into literature just by writing it down."

"Black ain't white and never can be. It is once and for only black. It ain't universal if that's what you are hintin up to. What I feel you feel different. You can't write about black because you don't have the least idea what we are or how we feel. Our feelin chemistry is different than yours. Dig that? It *has* to be so. I'm writin the soul writin of black people cryin out we are still slaves in this fuckn country and we ain't

gonna stay slaves any longer. How can you understand it, Lesser, if your brain is white?"

"So is your brain white. But if the experience is
about being human and moves me then you've made it
my experience. You created it for me. You can deny
universality, Willie, but you can't abolish it."

"Bein human is shit. It don't give you any privi-
leges, it never gave us any."

"If we're talking about art, form demands its rights,
or there's no order and maybe no meaning. What
else there isn't I think you know."

"Art can kiss my juicy ass. You want to know what's
really art? *I* am art. Willie Spearmint, *black man*. My
form is *myself*."

They faced each other, their eyes reflecting their
images, Willie fuming, Lesser cursing himself for having lost the morning.

"What a blackass fool I was to let you read my book."

Lesser desperately makes a final suggestion. "Why
don't you send your manuscript to a publisher and get
somebody else's opinion if you're not satisfied with
mine?"

"Because I tried ten of those rat-brained Jews
and they all turned it down for a lot of horseshit reasons, because they are *afraid* of what the book says."

The black, his eyes tumid, beats his head against
Lesser's wall, as the writer, not without pleasure,
looks on.

LESSER BEACHES HIS BATTERED RAFT.

A woman appears on the dunes.

Mirage, he mutters; but it's the real thing.

He leaves no footsteps following hers.

"If she be black and thereto have a wit,

She'll find a white that shall her blackness fit."

WILLIE SHAKESPEAR

Though he can't speak her language, nor clearly remember her face although he has invented it, they comprehend each other at a glance and are at once locked in four arms.

The lovers lie in the hot hungry grass, canaries flitting through the feathery palms above. Just as he is having it as he always hoped to with a black gal, a white hand touches his shoulder and he wakes against the will on this snowy cold morning in Manhattan, trying to remember if it was as good as they say.

Lesser hungers to sleep again and does for a change after awaking. Fog lifts on the beach. The sea at the

shore is green—purple beyond, the salt air warm,
ocean-fresh. In the distance clouds of islands float on
the swelling sea.

He finds her in the dunes, dancing to herself, her
nude blackness dancing in the dance.

As he runs to her a crow, cawing, with a rush of
wings swoops down between her legs and flies off with
a puff of black wool.

Holding her plucked member she curses the bird.

She curses Lesser.

Willie raps on the door.

"Lesser, I need my fuckn machine. I got to get on
to my work."

○

Willie, bleary, taut, suppressing rage, hauled out his
typewriter the morning after their unhappy talk and
did not return come siren, come noon. He didn't show
up that day or the next, Thursday. Lesser vaguely
worried but did not seek him out. Had he let a fellow
writer down? Said it wrong? Could he have put it
more tactfully? He had told Willie what he thought
he must but wondered if he mightn't have said it more
subtly, in a way that eased frustration and avoided
anger. He might have encouraged him more actively,
kept from hassling with him, gong to gong, though

that wasn't easy when you were dealing with a man whose writing wore his own thin skin, not to mention color.

After work Lesser went into the hall to Willie's office, listened at the door, heard nothing, peeked in. The table and chair were there but no sign of Willie Spearmint or his L. C. Smith. Harry wondered had he left the building for good. He searched through the flat, opening closets, and discovered the typewriter on the floor in the corner of the one in the bedroom. There it lay, vulnerable, unguarded. The writer figured Willie must still be upset, pissed off, else he would never have left it unprotected. He worried: Suppose some bum found it and dragged it off to a pawnshop? Unlike himself, who could get by with a pen, Willie, except for penciling in corrections, typed from first to last sentence. He said he thought better, typing. Lesser considered carting the machine into his place but wasn't sure Willie would appreciate that. When he comes back should I say he still ought to store it with me, or is he now and forever unwilling to accept the smallest favor from a white?

Should he forget it?

Over the weekend he forgot. Not totally. The thought of Willie's typewriter at times weighed in his head; but on the whole he forgot.

Monday morning he was in the thick of his long last chapter, stalking an idea that had appeared like a crack

in night pouring out daylight, Lesser trying with
twelve busy hands to trap the light—anyway, an exciting idea aborning that lit him like a seven-flamed
candle. At just that minute Willie ponderously kicked
the door. Boom, kick, boom. Lesser groaned as he ran
to open it. Willie entered, hauling in his machine, and
without explanation set it down under the table.

Welcome, Willie, I worried.

He was keeping his fingers in the flowering light,
trying to seize, hold it, while at the same time foresee-
ing what it might illuminate in time's every direction;
and memorize all this as he dealt with Willie.

Looking fully recovered except for a purple bruise
on his brow, the black laughed.

"Call me Bill, Lesser, man. My writing name is my
real one from now on I decided—Bill Spear."

Bill it was then, Lesser laughing self-consciously.

"I want to say something going back to our rap that
other day."

Exuding damp, the writer gave birth to several ex-
cuses why he couldn't just then listen, but could not
bring himself to utter them.

He cracked his knuckles.

"Won't take but a minute. All I want to tell you,
Lesser, is I went to the library where my chick's
house is near and took out your books. I borrowed them
both out. The second one gives off a bad smell"—he
held his broad-winged nose as Lesser felt himself blush

—"but that first one you wrote, man, I got to tell you it's a cool piece of work. After reading it, Irene said I was talking to myself. I tell you the Jesus truth, Lesser, I didn't expect it to be that good, not from the square dude you are."

Thanks anyway, Bill.

"Although I got some real reservations and one particular one."

Such as what?

"The black sister in that book, you don't touch her exactly right."

Lesser said she was a minor character he hadn't too much to say about.

"Like she ain't really black," Willie said, "not that chick, though I like her attitude. She has a whole lot of nature going for her and I wouldn't mind laying some pipe in her pants."

Wouldn't she be real if she got that kind of response from him?

"She's not like anybody real I know, leastways nobody black. In some of the ways she does things she might be white under that black paint you laid down on her."

Was it the white in the black that aroused him? No matter, Willie had liked the book.

Lesser glanced behind him as though expecting something he had left cooking to boil over and evaporate: He goes back to his desk, looks at the pages he had written that morning: not a visible word.

Willie looked too but went on talking, chop chop. A deep crease had appeared on his brow. He sighed, biffed one hand with the other, studied the scene outside the window, then turned to Lesser.

"Also I will admit it got me thinking. What I am thinking about after reading your book—both of them —is I understand a little different now some of those ideas you were preaching about form and that jazz, and which way it gives proportion to the writing. I also realize some things I could have done better in my book, and why I wasn't sure what was giving me the feeling of words and ideas shifting and moving after I thought I got them nailed down tight. In other words, Lesser, I am revising some of my thoughts and ideas about writing, though not all the way, don't get me wrong about that. But like I am thinking things through more than I did before on some of them."

Bravo, Willie—I mean Bill.

"What's the matter, man, don't you feel right?"

Lesser felt not too bad, he said.

"Got a belly cramp?"

No. Just something on his mind.

"What I said about revising some of my ideas don't mean I'm changing how I feel on black writing in comparison to white. Art is O.K. when it helps you to say what you got to, but I don't want to turn into a halfass white writer or an ass-kissing Neegro who imitates ofays because he is ashamed or afraid to be black. I write black because I am black and what I got to say means something different to black people than it does to whites, if you dig. We *think* different than you do, Lesser. We *do* and we *are,* and we *write* different. If some white prick tears a piece of black skin off your ass every day, when somebody says, 'Sit down,' it's gonna mean two different things to me and you, and that's why black fiction *has got* to be different than white. The words make it different because the experience does. You know that, man. Also we are the rising people of the future, and if the whites try to hold us down it ain't no secret we might have to cut your throats. You have had your day and now we are gonna have *ours.* That's what I got to write about but I want to write it in black art, in the best way I can. In other words, Lesser, I want to know what you know and *add on to that* what I know *because* I am black. And if that means I have to learn something from whitey to do it better as a black man, then I will *for that purpose only.*"

Bill blew his breath into one large fist, then the other. There were two creases on his brow.

He said he had decided to put aside the book Lesser

had read—he would work on it again later—and start something new with an idea that had been flapping around in the back of his mind since he was a kid trying to understand what his skin color had to do with why his life was so weird and crazy.

"It's about this black kid and his mama and how they burn off and work against each other till they kill themselves off, but not before—when this guy is a man—he goes out and gets him his revenge on the whites, maybe in some kind of riot, maybe in some personal way, because whitey is the real cause of his main troubles. Maybe he shoots twenty ofays before the pigs get to him. The point I am making, Lesser, in case you not with it, is I think this is the main way the blacks have to head along—to kill whites till those who are alive vomit with pain at the thought of what wrongs they have done us, and better not try to do any more. Now all I want you to do for me, Lesser, and I wouldn't be asking if we both wasn't writers, is not to spend any time criticizing the subject of any stuff I might show you, but to tell me the best way how I can write the same thing, with the same ideas, better. Only about the form of it, in other words, dig?"

Lesser, dreaming of new light in his book, beheld in his dark thoughts Bill Spear, potential executioner, requesting him to midwife his bloody fable.

He said he wondered whether that was such a good idea, considering how their talk had gone the other day. Subject and form were inseparable. Suppose he said something that was ultimately critical of an idea or two, would he have to worry he might have his throat cut?

Having said this he wished he hadn't. Not being able to get to work had set Lesser on edge.

"Baby," said Bill, in a sudden rage, "don't fuss your skull. If you don't want to read what I show you, fuck your bloody ass."

He slammed the door.

Lesser, momentarily relieved, returned to his desk to write a long note to himself about a new approach to his final chapter; but when he sat down he got up and followed the black back to his office.

He apologized for his impatience. It had caused him to express himself badly, Willie—I mean Bill. I think we can get along all right if your purpose is to improve the artistic quality of your work. Nobody says I have to love your ideas.

"I know your type, Lester."

Lesser explained he had been nervous about the loss of his writing time. On the other hand I want to help if I can because I respect your ambition to be the best writer you can be, I really do.

Bill quieted down.

"Now all I am asking you to do, Lesser, is after I get

a few chapters going along, to look at them and say *no more* than I am or I am not on the right track form-wise. You just say it and I'll be the one who makes up his own mind if you right. I don't plan to hang on to your tail for a free ride, you can bet your ass."

Lesser agreed to do his best if Bill was patient.

"And if you have a little bitsy of extra time," Bill said, wiping both palms on the apron of his overalls, "I want to catch up on some grammar—about noun clauses and such as that, even if nobody I know has much use for them. But I figure it won't hurt me to know about them though I don't want to do anything that will fuck up my own style. Like I like the way you write, Lesser, there's no crap in it, but I don't want to write like you."

Lesser said he would lend Bill a grammar. He could read it through and if he came across anything that interested him, they could talk it over after the day's work.

"Right on."

They shook hands.

"I like to bullshit with you, Lesser, you don't put on. We swinging real fine."

Lesser saw himself swinging.

He hurried at last back to his work. His inspired idea, possibly for an ending, whatever it might be, lay buried in an unmarked grave.

○

After Willie Spearmint became Bill Spear he added hours to his working hours. He no longer trudged into Lesser's flat at noon to put away his writing machine but appeared conveniently later, at three or half past three; and sometimes he sat late at his kitchen table, staring at the darkened sky. Lesser figured he was at work on his new book but did not know for sure because Bill said nothing and he would not ask him.

As for grammar, they talked once or twice about noun clauses, gerunds and gerundives, but the subject bored Bill. He said it killed the life out of language and never referred to it again. Instead, he studied his paperback dictionary, making lists of words in a notebook and memorizing their meanings.

After he knocked on Lesser's door in the afternoon, sometimes he stayed for a drink and they played records. The black responded to sound. As he listened his body spread an inch and his face took on an expression of repose and innocence. His protrusive eyes were shut and his lips tasted the music. But when Lesser put on his Bessie Smith, Bill, stretched out on the sofa, listened restlessly, squirming as though bitten by bugs.

"Lesser," he said in a slow burn, "why don't you give

that record away or break it up or eat it? You don't even know how to listen to it."

To avoid argument Harry said nothing. He removed the record from the turntable and replaced it with one of Lotte Lehmann singing Schubert lieder, which Bill, his stubby fingers locked on his chest, heard contentedly.

"Nice cat that Schubert," he said when the songs were sung. Then he rose, stretched his arms, wiggling his fingers, and yawned. He looked sadly at his face in Lesser's mirror and left.

"Jesus, man," he said the next afternoon, "how do you keep yourself working so fuckn long every day?"

"Same six hours daily," the writer replied. "I've done it for years."

"I thought it was more like ten. Yessir, looking at you I thought he's at it at least ten. Myself, I work close to seven now and hardly have time to wipe my ass. The worst about it is I don't want to do anything else but sit there and write. It's getting me scared."

Lesser said he wouldn't advise him to work his hours. A writer had to discover his own rhythm.

"Don't nobody have to tell me about rhythm."

"You might be more comfortable on your old schedule, quitting at noon."

"I don't appreciate you talking about quitting at the same time as I got my mind fixed on getting started."

His moist eyes reflected the windows.

"All I mean is my way of working isn't necessarily yours."

"What I like to know," Bill said, "is what do you get out of your life besides your writing? Like what do you do with your nature, man? Like with your meat tool? You got no girl, who do you fuck other than your hand?"

Lesser said he made out now and then. "Sometimes there are sweet surprises."

"I ain't talking about surprises. I am talking about life. What do you do for fun besides chess and push-ups?"

Less than he ought, Lesser admitted. He hoped for better once his book was done.

"With a decent advance I could maybe live in London or Paris for a year. But first I've got to do the kind of job I have to as an artist—I mean realize the potential of my book."

"You talk and you act like some priest or fuckn rabbi. Why do you take writing so serious?"

"Don't you?"

"Man, the way you go about it drags me to the ground." Bill began to shout. "You've bitched up and whammied all my pleasure that I used to enjoy out of my writing."

That night he moved a lumpy, urine-stained mattress into his office flat so that he could sleep over if he worked very late.

○

Here's Lesser enjoying Harlem.

He had asked Willie to go along to a restaurant for a soul-food meal of barbecued ribs, collard and kale, and sweet-potato pie; but the black said it was impossible, LIKE IMPOSSIBLE, so Lesser descended by parachute into Soul City by himself.

He sees himself walking on Eighth above 135th, drifting uptown alone on the wide dark sea, though the place is alive with many bright-sailed small craft and colored birds, brothers and sisters of all shades and shapes. Anyway, he is walking amiably along, not even thinking of writing, in love with the sights and sounds of this exotic small city on a warm and sunny day, waiting for somebody, blood or chick, young or old, to say as people once did in the not-so-long-ago-past, "Peace, brother, peace to you"; but nobody does, although this red-dress fat lady with an open-eyed dead plucked chicken in her string shopping bag laughs raucously when Lesser, lifting his straw skimmer, wishes her peace and prosperity for this and the coming year. The other passers-by either ignore him or cut The Man with scornful jibes:

Show-off cracker.

Ofay spy.

Goldberg hisself.

A stranger is a man who is called a stranger. Lesser, pleading innocence, makes hasty plans for departure.

It's then that Mary Kettlesmith, in an orange knitted mini way up her perfectly proportioned naked thighs, waltzes by in the company of Sam Clemence, a Mephistophelean type in yarmulke and yellow dashiki, who though he listens with head close to all the words they say has few of his own to offer.

Are you sportin tonight? Mary asks Lesser in a friendly way.

All the time, it relaxes me for writing. Too much work, too long, gets you uptight.

Black cunt, I mean?

Not that I would mind, Harry says.

Lemme see the color of your green.

Sam nods in grave agreement.

Money? Lesser turns pale. I was hoping to be invited out of friendship and affection.

Sam flips open his eight-inch mother-of-pearl switchblade, as Lesser, at his desk on Thirty-first near Third, brushes the reverie aside and returns to moving along his lonely sentences.

○

Although it was less than an hour after Bill had picked up his typewriter for another long day's banging that

Harry heard—and felt—a kick on his door one dreary February morning, the writer cursing fate, opened it expecting to see Bill's black head, but the big foot in the door and the cold eyes confronting Lesser's were unmistakably the pale-faced Levenspiel's.

"Who's the gorilla in Holzheimer's old flat? Friend of yours?"

"Which gorilla do you have in mind?"

"Don't play hard to get, Lesser," the landlord rumbled. "I found a typewriter there on the table in the kitchen. Also an apple less a few bites, and there's a piss-smelling mattress in the bedroom. Where's he hiding?"

Lesser opened the door wide.

Levenspiel, resting his meaty hand on the door frame, hesitated.

"I'll take your word but tell me who is this sonofabitch?"

"He comes and goes. Nobody I really know."

"He's some kind of a writer. I read a couple of the paper balls he rolls up and throws on the floor. One begins about a small boy in Harlem. Who is he, a colored?"

"I wouldn't know."

Levenspiel made a face.

"He's trespassing on private property, whoever he is. Tell him I'll throw him out on his ass."

Lesser said the landlord was trespassing on his writing time.

Levenspiel, still holding his foot athwart the threshold, softened his voice.

"So how's the work coming along?"

"On and off, too many interruptions."

"Would you consider $1,500 if I made you the offer, Lesser? Take it, it's pure gold."

Lesser said he would keep it in mind. Levenspiel, with a sigh, withdrew his foot.

"I won't repeat my troubles to you."

"Don't bother."

"You can imagine what I endure with three sick women around my neck, you're a writer, Lesser. You can appreciate the nasty little tricks of life, so yoishe, anyway, for Christ's sake. I can't go on like this forever. I'm not such a bad person. I beg you, yoishe."

"I'm writing as fast as I can. You push, you distort."

"So that's your final word?"

"Final once removed. What's final I seek but can't find. Maybe it's a blessing, I wish I knew."

Levenspiel then said sternly, "Tell your nigger friend I'm coming back with a cop."

"You tell him." Lesser shut the door.

He awaited the booming fist. Instead he heard the fire door slam. Stepping out in the hall, he listened, the heavy door held open a crack, until the landlord's flat footsteps had faded down the stairwell.

He looked into Bill's office. To his relief the L. C. Smith, a wordless sheet of pulpy, egg-yolk-yellow paper in its carriage, sat monumentally on the table. No doubt the weight of it had kept Levenspiel from hauling it down five flights, but he would surely send somebody up to grab it.

Harry carried the machine to his flat and laid it gently in the bathtub. He returned to search for a manuscript but there was none. Gathering up Bill's ream of new paper, his box of clips, pencil stubs and eraser, he also quickly stuffed some balls of paper, like overgrown bright yellow flowers on the floor, into his pants pockets.

Lesser returned to his study and picked up his fountain pen.

Bill knocked on the door, his face gray.

"I went out to find me a typewriter ribbon. Who took my stuff, you, Lesser?"

"Yes. Levenspiel found your setup and went out to get a cop."

"What the fuck for? What harm am I doing him?"

"Trespassing."

"In this smelly joint?"

"He had one writer to get rid of, now he's got two. There's a further indignity—you don't pay rent."

"Jew slumlord bastard."

"Shit with the Jew stuff, Willie."

"Bill is the name of my name, Lester," the black said, his eyeballs reddening.

"O.K., Bill, but cut out the Jew stuff."

Bill stared out the window. He turned to Lesser, his brow creased.

"What would you do if you was me?"

"Stay here," Lesser suggested. "Levenspiel's car is still parked across the street. Since you've got your typewriter here, why don't you go on with your work while I go on with mine? Use the kitchen table. I'll shut the door between us."

"I'm worrying about my desk and chair in my office. I don't want any trouble just now because the writing is beginning to roll along more lively. I would've had a great day's work if my typewriter ribbon hadn't got torn."

The fire door slammed. There were voices in the hall.

Lesser advised Bill to hide in the bathroom.

Bill, his throat cords taut, answered, "Not me, I ain't hiding anywheres."

Lesser whispered he had wanted to move the table and chair into another apartment but figured Levenspiel would hunt down the furniture if it had disappeared out of the room.

"I also thought of lugging it up to the roof."

"I appreciate your thoughts, Lesser."

"We're writers, Bill."

The black nodded.

A recognizable nightstick rat-tatted on the door.

"Open it up in the name of the law."

Bill slipped into Lesser's study.

The writer opened the door. "The bell still functions," he reminded Levenspiel. He asked the cop to state his business.

"Our business is legal," the landlord said. "We broke up your friend's furniture in the apartment where he was trespassing, but I know you are in possession of his typewriter that I already saw, Lesser."

"I hope you're proud of yourself."

"What are my rights, though they are rare for a landlord in this bastard city, are my rights. I doubt that I owe you any personal apologies, Lesser. Right now I'm about to search every goddamn apartment in the house and if I don't locate your black friend anywhere, then he's hiding here."

"Bring a search warrant if you want to get in."

"Damn right we will," said the young cop.

A half hour later, as Bill lay on the sofa with his hands clasped under his head, from his study window the writer watched Levenspiel drive off in his Oldsmobile. The cop remained across the street for an impatient ten minutes, then looked at his watch, threw a glance up at Lesser's window where he stood peeking behind the drawn green window shade, yawned, and sauntered off.

Bill and Lesser hurried to his office. When he beheld his smashed table and chair—they had pulled the legs off the table and broken up the chair—and his slashed mattress, Bill, jaw and lips tight, trembling, ultimately wiped his eye with his hand. Lesser, respecting his privacy, returned to his desk but was too disturbed to work.

Later he asked Bill what his plans were.

"I have no fuckn plans," he said bitterly. "My chick and I had a pissass flap and I ain't planning to go back there, leastways not just now."

"Work in my kitchen tomorrow," Lesser offered, overcoming indigenous reluctance. "Or if it makes you feel claustrophobic we can put the table in the living room."

"If you insist on it," said Bill.

Lesser slept badly that night. A guest forever is all I need. What is this strange curse on my book that I can't get the right conditions to finish it?

But in the morning he had made up his mind: do something about getting Bill another place to work. They ate breakfast. Bill, though disconsolate, devoured three eggs, a can of sardines, two cups of coffee with rolls, as Lesser downed a dish of oatmeal and a cup of black coffee. The writer suggested they search around in some of the second-hand furniture stores on Third Avenue and pick up a few necessary pieces for Bill.

"There's no bread in my pants, man. That's one of the things Irene and I were arguing about. Her new show is postponed and one of her nags on me, though her old man walks on bread, is to worry about when it's not coming in, and she keeps bugging me to get a gig. I told her, 'Sister, I have to start my new book off and I don't give a living shit who is slaving but it won't be me except on my writing.' I said if she was short on confidence in me I will find me another bitch."

"Forget about money. I still have a few bucks in my bank account."

"That's fine and dandy of you, Lesser, but could we take the chance of putting another table and chair in just after this bust? Suppose those birdturds come back here today?"

Lesser agreed. "Let's wait a day or two and meanwhile you work here and I'll work at my desk."

"Right on."

Two difficult days later, neither Levenspiel nor the cop having returned to the hunt, they bought Bill an unfinished maple table, a cane-bottom, solid black chair, a folding cot, and a tasseled, old-fashioned floor lamp with a marble base. Lesser tried to persuade him to move down a floor or two but he objected because there was no view lower down.

"What view is there up here?"

"I like to look at the roofs, man."

He was, however, willing to move across the hall into Mr. Agnello's former flat that had the toilet that sometimes flushed.

They carried the new furniture up the stairs during the evening, with the assistance of Sam Clemence and a friend of his, Jacob 32, a modest gent, Bill said, though Lesser was not comfortable in his presence. Jacob 32, who had uneasy eyes and a pencil-line mustache, was not comfortable in Lesser's presence.

They swept and mopped up the rooms with Lesser's broom and wet mop. The writer also gave Bill a worn afghan for his cot.

The next afternoon they found a typed notice pasted on Holzheimer's door: NO TRESPASSING OR ILLEGAL ENTRY UNDER PENALTY OF ARREST! IRVING LEVEN-SPIEL, OWNER!

The landlord fortunately had not looked into Agnello's apartment. But after that, Bill, worrying about his new possessions, agreed to move down to a not-bad back flat on the fourth floor, the opposite corner from Lesser's. He and the writer hauled down the furniture. Bill wrote busily every day, including Sundays, but after another week he and Irene made up and he returned to her apartment, though only for weekends.

"Like I concentrate better when I don't see her during the week," Bill told Harry. "I got my first chapter in the breeze at last. If you see cunt you want cunt though she is pissing a lot lately so it ain't that much of a problem."

"Pissing?"

"She's got cystitis and you can't ball them then or the germs might penetrate in you and then you have to piss all day."

"Really?"

"That's what I hear. Irene has this on and off. It started when she was a little chick. She has that and some other hangups I got to be patient with, but that's the nature of her nature."

"What sort of hangups?"

"She was a fucked-up nigger-struck chick when I took her on. She had nothing she believed in herself. I straightened her out in the main ways because I gave her an example, that I believed in my blackness."

"What does she believe in now?"

"Me more than herself, and sometimes she believes in God, which I don't."

He said nothing more about her.

"I'm writing hard," he told Lesser. He wore wire-framed, blue-tinted granny glasses and had grown a bushy mustache to go with his goatee.

Bill had nailed up pictures of W. E. B. Du Bois,

Malcolm X, and Blind Lemon Jefferson on the wall of his new kitchen-office. It wasn't a bad place to work, Lesser thought, though it looked a little barren and wasn't so well daylit as the upstairs place. A wash of shadow hung in the light.

Although Lesser feared it would not be long before Levenspiel chanced on Bill's new furniture, he left a bottle with six red-and-white carnations in it on a shelf in his new office.

"Luck with your new book," he wrote in large letters on a sheet of typing paper. Partly he left the flowers in relief to have Bill out of his flat. Lesser felt he hadn't worked in an age.

Bill, perhaps embarrassed by the carnations, said nothing in the way of thanks for anything, except once he remarked there might be a diddle of black in Lesser's blood.

In the Babylonian past a black slave socks it to a white bitch from the Land of Israel?

○

Bill insisted on showing the writer the first chapter of the novel he had recently begun. Lesser asked him not to just yet, but Bill said it would help him know if he had started off right. He said this was a brand-new book although there were some scenes from the other novel, brought from Mississippi to Harlem, where most of the action would take place. Bill asked Lesser to read the chapter in his presence. He sat in Harry's armchair, wiping his glasses and looking at a newspaper on his knees as the writer, chain-smoking, read on the sofa. Once Harry glanced up and saw Bill sweating profusely. He read quickly, thinking he would lie if he didn't like the chapter.

But he didn't have to. The novel, tentatively called *Book of a Black*, began in Herbert Smith's childhood. He was about five in the opening scene, and nine at the end of the chapter; but in truth he was an old man.

In the opening scene, one day the boy drifted out of his neighborhood into a white neighborhood and couldn't find his way home. Nobody spoke to him except an old white woman who saw him through her ground-floor window, sitting on the curb.

"Who are you, little boy? What's your name?"

The boy wouldn't say.

In the afternoon this old-smelling white woman came out of the house and took the boy by the hand to the police station.

"Here's a boy that's lost," she said.

He wouldn't answer the white pigs when they asked him questions. Finally they sent in a black cop to find out where he belonged.

"Can't you talk, boy?"

The boy nodded.

"Then talk and tell me where do you live at."

The boy wouldn't answer.

The black cop got him a glass of milk to drink, then lifted the boy into his car and drove into Harlem. They walked from street to street, the policeman asking people sitting on the stoops if they knew this kid. No one did. Finally a fat black woman, fanning herself though the day was cool, said she did. She led them two blocks up the street to the tenement where she said the boy lived.

"Do you live in this here house?" asked the cop.

"He sure do," said the fat woman.

The boy said nothing.

"You sure are a terror," said the cop. "If you was mine I would blast you ass."

In a flat on the top floor of the house they found the mother drunk in bed. She was naked but did not pull up the blanket.

"Is this you boy?"

She turned her head and wept.

"I asked you to tell me is this you boy?"

She nodded and wept.

The cop left the boy there and went downstairs.

The woman wept.

The boy smeared a slice of stale bread with some rancid lard and went down to the street to eat it.

In the last scene of the chapter the mother has a visitor who drops in every other night.

. . . He was an ofay who liked to pretend to talk nigger talk. It made him feel good to do it though it was fake black talk. He did not come from the South, he came from Scranton, Pa. He came to my mama because she charged one dollar and it wasn't before long that he used to get it for free. And also my mama did all the things he wanted her to do. Sometimes he left us a loaf of sandwich bread on the table or a can of pears, or string beans, or mushy canned fruit. I remember he left a can of tomato paste that my mama smeared on the bread and gave it to me to eat. Sometimes he also gave her two packs of Lucky Strikes. My mama was about twenty-seven years then and I was nine years old. On the street they called this guy "Rubber Dick." He was a tall stringy Charlie with long legs and a big prick. He liked to take it out and show it to me and scare me off. I hated him and had thoughts to kill him off with my zip gun but was afraid to. I told my mother to warn him to stay out of the house but she said she didn't mind having him for company.

"Is he comin here tonight?" I asked her.

"Well, he jus might."

"I hope he dies before he gets here. I hope I kill him if he comes in this here room."

"I gon wash your mouth with soap if you say that word again."

"I got nothin to be shame of."

"He treats me real fine. Las week he buy me a pair of pretty shoes."

I know he didn't buy her no shoes.

I left the house but when I came back to eat some supper, he was there, smoking a Lucky Strike cigarette.

"Wheah at is Elsie?" he asked me in nigger talk and I said I didn't know.

He looked at me in a way that was supposed to witch me and he sat on the bed with a shit smile on his mouth.

"I gon wait for her."

He told me to come over to him on the bed, he wouldn't hurt me.

I was scared so nauseous I thought if I moved one teensy bit I would crap in my pants. I wanted my mother to come back fast. If she came back I would not mind what they did to each other.

"Come heah, boy, and unzip mah pants."

I told him I didn't want to.

"Heah's a nice tin cints piece you kin have."

I didn't move at all.

"Heah's a quotah mo. Now unzip mah pants and the money is yo's. Bof the dime and the quotah."

"Don't take it out, please," I asked him.

"Not till you show me kin you open yo mouf wide an covah yo teef wif yo lips like this."

He showed me how to cover my teeth.

"I will do it if you stop talking nigger talk to me."

He said honey he would, and also I was a smart boy and he loved me very much.

He was talking like a whitey again.

Lesser said it was a strong chapter and praised the writing.

"How is the form of it?"

"It's well formed and written." He said no more than that, as they had agreed.

"Damn right, man. It's strong black writing."

"It's well written and touches the heart. That's as much as I'll say now."

Bill said that in the next chapter he wanted to get deep into the boy's black consciousness, already a fire of desire and destruction.

He lived that day in a potless triumphant high.

That night both writers, over water glasses filled with red wine, talked about being writers and what a good and great thing it was.

Lesser read aloud a passage he had written in a notebook: "I am convinced more and more day by day that fine writing is next to fine doing the top thing in the world."

"Who said that?"

"John Keats, the poet."

"Fine dude."

"And here's something from Coleridge: 'Nothing can permanently please which does not contain in itself the reason why it is so and not otherwise.' "

"Copy that down for me, man."

○

Depressed, one useless morning, dispossessed of confidence in himself as writer, as he sometimes was, Lesser, shortly before noon at the Museum of Modern Art, stood before a painting of a woman done by a former friend of his, a painter who had died young.

Although he had sat at his desk for hours, that day for the first time in more than a year Lesser had been unable to write a single sentence. It was as though the book had asked him to say more than he knew; he could not meet its merciless demands. Each word weighed like a rock. If you've been writing a book for ten years time adds time to each word; they weigh like rocks—the weight of waiting for the end, to become the book. Though he struggled to go on, every thought, every decision, was impossible. Lesser felt depression settle on his head like a sick crow. When he couldn't write he doubted the self; this expressed itself in reservations about the quality of his talent—was it really talent, not an illusion he had dreamed up to keep himself writing? And when he doubted the self he couldn't write. Sitting at his desk in the bright morning light, scanning yesterday's pages, he had felt about to throw up: language, form, his plan and purpose. He felt sick to death of the endless, uncompleted, beastly book, the discipline of writing, the overdedicated, ultimately limited, writer's life. It needn't be so but was for Lesser. What have I done to myself? So much I no longer see or feel except in language. Life once removed. So against the will he had taken the morning off and gone for a walk in the February sun. Lesser tried to put his thoughts out of mind as he walked. He named his unhappiness "depression," and let it go at that; for though he presently resisted everything concerned with writing he could not forget he wanted more than anything else to write a fine book.

It was a warmish cold day of snow melting, and he drifted aimlessly uptown, pretending not to be thinking of his work, whereas in desperate truth he was scribbling away in the head—it came to not much. Though the writer was not crippled he walked with a limp. He saw with a limp, nothing quite meets his gloomy gaze or fastens there. He is missing something —that begins in an end. He thinks of settlement, compromise, a less than perfect conclusion—how many will know the difference? But when he sneaks around his malaise and sees himself once more at his desk, writing, he can't imagine he will settle for less than a sufficient ending, the one that must be if the book is to be as good as it must. Anyway, Lesser, after a dozen blocks, admits that whatever presently afflicts him is not an incurable disease. A man is entitled to be momentarily fed up. All he has to do to scare the puking bird off his skull, dispel the despondency that keeps him from working, is go back to his desk and sit down with his pen in his hand; asking not what the writing will or won't give him. So it's not the whole of life but who holds the whole of life in his two hands? Art is an essence, not of everything. Tomorrow is a new day; finish the book and the day after comes bearing gifts. If he began once more to work, settled, calm, *at it,* the mysterious ending, whatever it was or might be, would come of itself as he worked. My God, here it is on paper. He could not conceive how else it would come. No angel flies into his room with a scroll revealing the mystery baked into a loaf of bread, or hidden in a mezuzah. One day he would write a word, then another, and the next is the end.

But the longer Lesser walked the winter streets, the less he felt like returning home and at last gave up the struggle and decided to take a holiday. Big laugh if holiday comes by default. You couldn't do—for whatever confused reason—what you wanted most to do, ought this minute to be doing, for in essence the job was almost done—hadn't he invented every step that led to an

end? Hadn't he written two or three endings, a com-
bination of endings? You had only to choose the right
one and put it down once and for all; perhaps it needed
one final insight. Then you could, after the book was
there, reconsider your life and decide how much of the
future you wanted to invest in writing—something
less than past investment of time and toil. He was
tired of loneliness, had thoughts of marriage, a home.
There was the rest of one's life to live, uncertain but
possible, if you got to it. Harry promised himself to
take at least a year off after finishing this book before
beginning another. And the next would go three years
in the writing, not seven, not longer. Ah, well, that's
the future, what do you do with a holiday? Since it has
been months that he had stepped into a gallery and
prowled amid pictures, Lesser, on Fifty-third Street,
walked west to the Museum of Modern Art, and after
wandering through the permanent collection not
really looking—he found it hard to be attentive—
stopped in the last room, before his former friend's
abstract and fragmented "Woman."

Lazar Kohn, an inscrutable type, had been a friend
of Lesser's for a short time in their early twenties. He
had become successful too soon for the continuance
of their friendship—while the future writer was hating
himself for not having yet begun. After a while Kohn
stopped seeing him; Lesser, he said, spoiled his pleas-

ure in his triumph. When Lesser's first novel appeared, Kohn was abroad; when his second was published, Kohn was dead. His motorcycle had crashed, one rainy night, into a huge moving van on Hudson Street. His work, it was said, had been going badly.

There was his green-and-orange picture: a woman trying to complete herself through her own will, as willed by the painter. Otherwise she was an appearance of a face and body trying to make it through a forest of binding brush strokes.

The portrait of the woman—Lesser had once met the model at a party but nothing had come of it—had never been completed. Kohn had worked on it for years and then given up. Lesser had learned this from the model, Kohn's one-time mistress. Kohn, in defeat, after all his labor, doubt, despair he was not making it, nor ever would, had turned the unfinished canvas to the wall; she had eluded him. You work as you always have but with this picture for no reason you can give or guess, except that it means so much to you to do it as it should be done, you can't this time make it. She isn't what I hoped she might be. Whoever she is I don't know and want no further part of. Let time fuck her, I can't. But friends who had seen the portrait in Kohn's studio, in various aspects and colors, said the painter had "made it" despite himself, whether he thought so or no; it was accomplished as art whether or not accomplished as subject, or as originally conceived. Whatever he put his hand to was Lazar Kohn and Kohn was a distinguished painter. His friends persuaded him to release the picture to his gallery for sale. The museum had bought it and hung it in its permanent collection.

The picture deepened Lesser's dejection. Why had it been abandoned? Who knows?—like Lesser, Kohn had had his hangups. Maybe he had wanted to say more than he could at that time, something that wasn't then in him to say? He might have said it after the motorcycle accident, if he had survived. Or had he been unable to separate the woman from who she really was: she had as self got the better of his art? He could not invent beyond her? She was simply the uncompleted woman of an incomplete man because it was that kind of world, life, art? I can't give you more than I have given you—make you more than you are—because I haven't presently got it to give and don't want anyone to know, least of all myself. Or perhaps it was the painter's purpose to complete by abandoning, because abandonment or its image was presently a mode of completion? Peace to Valéry. In painting, Lesser thought, you could finish off, total up, whether done or undone, because in the end (the end?) you hung a canvas object on the wall and there was no sign saying, "Abandoned, come back tomorrow for more." If it hung it was done, no matter what the painter thought.

Thinking of his own work, regretting that he had never been able to talk with Kohn about it, Lesser reflected that if he could not complete his novel; in the end something essential missing—the ending—some act or appearance or even promise of resolution, hence the form unachieved; then it was no completed work of art, did not deserve to be a book—he would destroy it himself. Nobody would read it except those who already had—besides himself perhaps some bum who had fished a few pages of a prior draft out of the garbage can in front of the house, curious to know what the words said. Lesser then vowed, as he often had, that he would never abandon this novel, never, for whatever reason; nor would anybody good or bad, Levenspiel, Bill Spear, for instance, or any woman, black or white, persuade him to give it up; or call the job done before he had completed it. He had no choice but to bring his book to its inevitable and perfected end.

Who says no?

○

As Lesser leaves the last gallery, wondering what would happen if he went home and picked up his pen, a blue-hatted black woman in the lobby drops a mirror out of her cloth handbag and it shatters on the floor. A girl in a voluminous silk-lined black cape coming out of the ladies' room quickly walks away from it. Lesser, stooping, hands the black woman a large triangular sliver of glass. In it he sees himself, unshaven, gloomy, gaunt; it comes from not writing. The black woman spits on the fragment of mirror Lesser has given her. He backs off. Lesser hurries after the girl in the cape into the street. He had often thought of her, sometimes while writing.

"Shalom," he says in the street.

She looks at him oddly, coldly. "Why do you say that?"

He fumbles, says he isn't sure. "I never use the word."

Irene, a moody type, walks in noisy boots along the slushy sidewalk, going towards Sixth Avenue, Lesser walking along with her, surprised to be though he invents surprises of this sort easily enough in his fiction. She moves with a loose-limbed, slightly pigeon-toed stride, wearing a knitted green wool hat from which her hair pours down her back. Her intricate earrings clink faintly. Lesser is thinking of her as she looked at his party—her short thick skirt and pink blouse, her plump white breasts; of looking up her legs to the conjoining thighs. He remembers her dance with Bill he hadn't been able to break into.

She's a black man's girl, they're a special breed. I'm on my way home.

"How about coffee?" Irene asks.

He says fine.

They sit at a counter. She holds the hot cup with both hands to warm her nail-bitten fingers. Her eyes are evenly green and blue. Her black hair, in daylight, is golden blond.

Lesser, as they drink their coffee, waits as though expecting a confession but she makes none.

He tries to breathe in her perfume but the scent is hidden. Behind the ears? Under her long cape? In her sweaty armpits? Between breasts or legs? He has made the grand tour but hasn't sniffed flowers. No gardenia, no garden.

"Don't you have a girl?"

He asks why she asks.

"You had nobody for yourself at your party."

"The last girl I had was about a year ago. I had one the summer before that. They get impatient waiting for me to finish my book."

"Willie says it's taking forever."

"I'm a slow writer. It's my nature."

She smiles sourly.

"Let's get out of here," Lesser says.

They walk up Sixth to the park, dirty with melting snow, the pale dead grass on hard ground visible in dark circles under trees. They stand by the low stone wall on Fifty-ninth, overlooking the snowy meadow. The park is of diminished reality to Lesser, tight, small, remote. The book he is writing is unbearably real in his thoughts. What am I doing so far away from it? What am I doing here on a working day in the middle of winter?

"When do you laugh?" she says. "You're so deadly serious. It's your fucking book."

"I laugh when I write," Lesser says. "I haven't written a word today. I ought to be writing now."

"Why aren't you?"

Lesser sees himself leaving her at the wall. He crosses Fifth and heads for Third. Halfway to Madison he stops, experiencing a sense of loss. What a fool I am, he thinks. He walks back to where he has left Irene. He thinks she won't be there but she is. She's standing at the wall in a long cape, like a bird about to fly off.

"Why is it taking so long?"

He says he doesn't want to talk about it.

"Is it still that book about love?"

"That's the book," he says.

"I read your first novel. Willie got it out of the library and gave it to me after he finished it. It's very good, better than I thought it would be. The girl reminds me of myself when I was her age. I don't like her. Did you have anyone real in mind?"

Lesser says no.

They sit on a bench.

"You're all such self-conscious characters," Irene says. "When Willie's hung up on his writing he's awful to live with. He fights all the minutes of the day. It's hard to take."

Again the small smile as she inspects her pigeon toes.

"It was bad enough for him but you've made it worse. He was awfully hurt by your criticism of his book."

"I didn't want to hurt him."

"He said you didn't think much of it."

"I like the stories better than the Life. They're a lot more original."

"It isn't just autobiography. Willie came from Georgia to Harlem with his mother and kid sister when he was sixteen."

"I thought it was Mississippi."

"He changes his birthplace every time he talks about it. I think he hates to remember it."

"There's a lot he hates to remember. Did he serve a stretch in prison?"

"Two years. But a lot of the book is made up. Willie's an imaginative guy. He enjoys being imaginative. You should hear him when he gets talking about himself. That's the tone I'd like to see in his book. Do you like what he's writing now?"

"So far," says Lesser.

"Do you think he is a good writer—I mean will he be?"

"He is though not consistently. If he stays with it seriously he ought to be good."

"How seriously? Like you have to break your balls to be a writer?"

"There's no halfass way to be a good writer."

"There's nothing halfass about Willie."

Lesser asks her how she and Willie stand as of now.

She strikes a match, then finds she has no cigarette.

"What do you mean?"

"You seem to be together but you seem to be apart."

"That's a good description of us."

"It's none of my business," Lesser says.

"If you say that it means you think it is."

He says he wishes it were.

"I'm not objecting to your question. I'm wondering how to answer it."

"Don't if you don't want to."

"Willie and I met about three years ago—that was about a year and a half after I'd quit college to try being an actress. Not that I was that much of one but the idea of it had become an obsession. My God, what a batty girl I was, and I weighed a good twenty-five more pounds than I do now. I'm not bad in my performances but I can't go down low enough when I have to, or up as high as I would like to. What I'm saying is I wanted to act mainly so that I could skip being myself. A lot of this came out in my analysis. I wasn't very self-knowing."

"You look like an actress but you don't playact."

"I used to an awful lot. Anyway, what it amounted to is acting as a means of getting away from myself. I was a fucked-up kid, I drew men like flies and slept around till I began to wake up frightened."

It seems to Lesser he had left his room that morning to hear her talk about herself.

"I had a very rough time for over a year—but never mind that. I met Willie and we began to see each other. The blackness of him scared and excited me. I asked him to live with me. I was beginning to be in love with him and I also wanted to know if I could be faithful to one guy. Anyway he moved into my apartment. He wasn't writing as steadily as he is now— for a while he was hung up on whether it was going to be revolution or soul, and I don't really think he's resolved that. He used to write only when he felt he had to. At first we got along badly, then we got kinder to each other and began to have a better time all around. Certain things eased up in me. They stopped being so important—like acting, because I began to have a realer understanding of myself and I don't want to be a halfass anything. And I told you I'm in analysis, which I couldn't bring myself to do before I met Willie."

"Do you love him?"

Irene's eyes are suddenly hungry. "Why do you want to know?"

"Because we're sitting here."

She flips the matchstick into the snow.

"Outside of his love for black people I don't really think he loves anything but his work. Otherwise I think we'd've been married by now. Willie was always conscious of his color but it's more so now. The more he writes the blacker he becomes. We talk an awful lot about race and color. A white chick is no longer such a hot thing for a black man, especially the activists. Willie won't let me hold his hand in public any more. Just when I thought there was a chance we might get married he began to say, 'I'll tell you the truth, Irene, my writing doesn't come on right with me living with a white chick.' I said to him, 'Willie, do what you want to, I have only so much energy.' He moved out of the apartment for a while, then one night he called me up and moved back in. Now it's just a weekend deal till he really gets into his book, he says."

Lesser says nothing. What she has told him has set off an excitement. He feels in himself a flow of language, a surge of words towards an epiphany.

"What about you?" she says. "I told you about me."

He rises craving to write.

"Do you want to walk any more?" Irene asks. Her eyes are vague, unsure. She opens her purse and roots around for something she can't find, maybe a mirror. Lesser thinks of Lazar Kohn's "Woman."

"One thing about loving a black man," Irene says, "there are times you feel black yourself."

In that case find yourself another.

The writer says he has his work to get back to.

○

February had stepped aside to let a whiff of leaf and flower into present time. Tomorrow will again be winter; in the meantime this puff of promised spring tormented Lesser.

The writer, alone, this end-of-February night, heading downtown on the east side of Lexington for no other reason than that he had walked uptown on the other side last night, heard laughter across the street and recognized, amid the stream of people passing by, Bill Spear with Irene Bell. They were at the head of a small parade within the Friday night crowd moving along on the sidewalk; behind them was Sam Clemence and behind him four other blacks walking in pairs: a small neatly dressed brown man wearing a big-brimmed black velours hat, with a heavy, light-skinned, fur-coated woman holding his arm; then two iron-bearded black men in long cloth coats, one carrying a flute case, the other a bongo drum he tapped as he walked. The man with the bongo had a broken nose taped with adhesive.

Lesser, recognizing four of the seven and hearing their laughter, felt longing invade his gut and began to follow them. As he watched Irene with Bill, both enjoying themselves, his feeling turned unpleasant, desire in corrosive emptiness, intensified by shame for feeling as he felt. Could I be jealous of them? How can that be if I have nothing to be jealous of and am not, so far as I know, a jealous type? Recalling that he had experienced a similar seizure on first seeing Irene at his party, something more than hunger touched with regret that he hadn't got to her before Willie had, Lesser felt a disquietude so strange he had to stop a minute to brace himself against a lamppost.

From across the street near a florist shop Bill spied him and whooped, "Lesser, man, for Christ's sake, cross on over here. I got some soul people with me."

Lesser, struggling to settle his confused state, waved, and stepped into the street, bucking the light in heavy traffic as the blacks and Irene watched with interest to see if he would make it. Eventually he did, hiding his uneasy excitement, trying not to reveal himself to Irene, who was distantly observing him with eyes wondering why he had appeared, if not who was he.

If you swim the Hellespont where there is none, what are you trying to tell yourself? Or anybody else?

"We are partying at Mary's pad," Bill said. "How do you like to come along?"

Lesser said he wouldn't mind.

"Join the train."

Harry glanced at Irene as though for her sanction but she was already walking on.

"What for this ofay type?" Sam asked Bill, loud enough for Lesser to hear.

"He is a fuckn good writer in one of his books and you were there when he laid down his bread for my furniture that's in my office now."

"Join the train," he called.

None of the pairs made room for one more abreast and Lesser preferred not to walk with Sam, so he tailed the line to Mary's. He had met only one of the four people in the rear, the man with the light-skinned woman, Jacob 32, who nodded gravely with both eyes shut. The others ignored him but Lesser was glad to be with them, even as caboose to their train. The jealousy that had invaded him had vanished and he enjoyed the promise of spring in the February night.

○

Mary lived in a psychedelically painted loft with a girl-friend who was an illustrator. She said she was happy to see Lesser. Who was happy to see him Lesser was happy to see.

"I thought you might come around sometime," Mary said, "seeing we live so close by. My phone is in the book."

He said he had thought of it. "I thought of it the other night, then I remembered that smell that bothered you last time."

"Oh I was zonked that night," she laughed, touching Lesser's arm. "You shouldn't have held back or felt shy."

"Are you zonked now?"

"I'm staying off grass. When I'm high on it I get low."

As she spoke she watched his eyes. "Are you partial on Irene? You been eye-eating her."

"She's Bill's girl."

"Your eyes stay soft on her."

"It's her mini, I like those long legs."

"Mine are better shaped."

Lesser agreed. "You're a good-looking woman, Mary." In a moment of loneliness and daring, he said to her, "If you liked me I could give you back affection."

Mary, her neck arched, blinked both eyes and walked away.

I write it right but say it wrong, Lesser thought. I write it right because I revise so often. What I say is unrevised and often wrong. Then he thought, I write about love because I know so little about it.

There were about twenty souls at the party, the writer and Irene the only whites. White souls? Four of the brothers sat barefoot on the floor, improvising black sound with a heartrending beat. Above them rocked a fifth musician with his bull fiddle. Everybody else was dancing, rocking. As he listened to the music the writer felt a yearning, longing for life. The brother with the taped nose beat his bongo with eyes shut. His twin, flowers woven into his stiff beard, played his flute high and sweet. One man plucked the strings of a twelve-string guitar, listening privately to each sound. A brother wearing a gold blouse and red fez beat a rhythmic spoon on an empty bottle. The standing brother, rapping his fingers on his booming bass fiddle, hugged and swayed with it. Each of them whipped up an island of sound around himself. They played to each other, saying their music was beautiful and so were they. Over them hung an umbrella of sweet smoke, and Lesser felt high.

Feeling high, he asked Irene to dance but she was

engaged with Sam, who said he didn't appreciate being cut in on. Irene shrugged in mock frustration but said nothing. Lesser thought of the jealousy he had felt before. A short aberration, he thought, directed nowhere in particular, just pro-desire. Bill, in yellow cords, purple silk shirt, short brown boots and a flowered headband, circled Mary, boogalooing. Irene, in an orange mini, was dancing barefoot, her narrow feet honest, her face flushed. She abandoned Sam as Bill left Mary. They bopped in unison like contrasting birds, each dancing in his casual, habitual orbit as though forever. Bill smiled benignly at his bitch and Irene gazed at him with sad affection. They looked like married folk.

Mary danced with Sam, who shimmied high and shimmied low. Sam moved like a stork with palsy, Mary, both arms aloft, danced with hot eyes. At last she left Sam to dance with Harry.

"Listen now," Mary said as they stepped and twisted, "I got the door key to a friend's apartment across the hall. As soon as people get a little more high I will go on in there and you come in if you have the mood to. Only give me ten more minutes of time so nobody sees us going out of here one right after the other, or Sam might feel bad."

"All right," Lesser said. "But don't get zonked before you go in."

"Okay now. I'll do like you say, honey."

Harry ducked, swung his arms, stepped to the beat of the music as Mary Kettlesmith, in a short slender white-green-and purple striped dress danced exotically around him.

She soon slipped out of the loft, Lesser's anticipation rising, his throat dry. Bill, he saw, looked bleary —tonight he was drinking. Irene was in and out of the bathroom, still with cystitis?

The writer, after a quarter of an hour, stepped into the barren outer hall and entered the one-room apartment across from Mary's loft, his heartbeat shaking his frame. Mary lay waiting in bed, covered with a rose blanket. A canary flitted on a bar in a cage by the window.

"Do you mind me getting undressed first? The room is cold and I thought it would be warmer waiting in bed."

Lesser lifted the blanket for a look at her.

"My God, you're lovely."

"Tell me what you like."

"Your breasts and belly. The black of you." He passed his hand over her velvet skin.

"Haven't you had a black woman ever?"

"No."

"Don't make too much out of it. Come on in bed now, honey," she said.

When he had undressed and got under the covers

with her, Mary said, "Lesser, I want to tell you something. My doctor says I am built a little small. You have to go easy not to hurt me at first."

He said he'd be gentle.

"If you would."

They embraced. Her fingers moved over his face, then down his side and between his legs. He touched her breasts, soft belly, and felt the wet between her thighs.

Mary put out the lamp.

"Don't," said Lesser.

She laughed and put it on.

Sweating lightly, moaning to herself, after a while Mary said, "You better come on and come, I don't think I will make it, Harry."

"Is it some smell of me?"

"No smell at all."

"Try. I'll hold a while."

For a time she tried with him. Then Mary said with a sigh, "I'm not going to make it at all. You better come on now."

"Did you drink much tonight?"

"Only one scotch and part of another. I didn't take a thing after you said not to."

"I'd like it better if you came too."

"So would I but you better go on alone. I will help you if you tell me what you want me to do."

"Just stay with me," said Lesser.

He came with pleasure, cupping her buttocks. Mary kissed him affectionately. "Lay on me for a while, it keeps me warm." She entwined both arms around him.

Lesser lay on her half asleep. "This is good, Mary."

"I'm sorry I didn't come along with you."

"Don't worry about it."

"Just I like you and would like to come along."

"Next time," Lesser said.

Later, after she had gone to the bathroom, she hung a string of green and violet beads around his neck.

"What's this for?"

"For our luck," said Mary. "Okay now?"

They lay in bed, passing a cigarette back and forth.

He asked her whether she had ever come with anybody.

"I huff and puff with Sam to make him feel good but I don't really think I have."

He said she would.

"I almost did with you."

"How long haven't you?"

"I don't want to think about that."

"Do you have any idea why you don't?"

"Unless it was because I was raped when I was little, which happened to me on the cellar stairs after he dragged me down there."

"Jesus—who?"

"This redhead nigger neighbor boy from upstairs. His daddy was white and beat the shit out of his black mother. My mama said it got the boy so frustrated he hated everybody and wanted to hurt them. He finally got sent away."

"Tell me, Lesser," said Mary after a while, "do your girls come all of the time?"

"Most of the time."

"Do they come more than once?"

"One used to."

"The bed is not my most favorite place," she said.

"Are you crying, Mary?" Lesser asked.

"No, sir, I am not."

"It sounds as though you were."

"That's not me. Usually it's Sam out in the hall, kneeling by the keyhole and crying," Mary said.

○

"A Salaam Aleikum," Jacob 32 said to Lesser when he returned to Mary's loft. Mary had gone back first. Jacob was a narrow-eyed man in a dark blue suit. His gaze locked with Lesser's, but he spoke gently, as though he had been asked to.

"If you think you white you wrong," said Jacob. "You really black. The whites are black. The blacks are the true white."

"I think I know what you mean."

"No, you don't. You see us wrong and you see your-self wrong. If you saw me right you would see me white in the manner which I see you black. You think I am black because your inside eyes are closed to the true vision of the world."

Lesser said no more.

"This is a eye-to-eye confrontation of the force of evil versus a vessel of good," said Jacob 32, "and it ain't up to me to reveal to you which is the which."

○

Mary had locked herself in her bathroom and Lesser was left alone with a crowd of silent blacks. He guessed that Sam had told them and nobody cared for the news. Irene was standing at a dark window in the loft, looking out, her face haunted in the glass. Lesser saw himself in it, staring at her.

We're both scared but what is she scared of?

Bill Spear, his mouth slack, heavy eyes glazed, drunk but steady on his feet, summoned Lesser from across the room. Beside him stood Sam Clemence, thick-calved in striped bell-bottoms, aloof but mourn-ing. A cluster of blacks with inexpressive faces was massed around them.

"Lesser, move your paleface ass on over here."

Now I take my lumps, he thought. Maybe for not

satisfying Mary. Maybe that's the name of the game. The stranger who fails is a dead duck. It's an ancient entrapment and I shouldn't have played. I'm too young to be the sacrifice in a stomp-in. He was alarmed by the thought of broken fingers and bloody eyes.

Bill's flushed eyes were sullen. Of the blacks he was the blackest present.

"Chum," he said, tapping his stubby finger against Lesser's noisy chest, "we have a game we got we call the dozens. Like the brothers play it no ofay has that gift or the wit, and also since whitey ain't worth but half a black I'm gon play you the half-dozens. Now it's a game of nothin but naked words. I'm gon do mine on you and you do yours on me, and the one who bleeds, or flips, or cries mama, he's the loser and we shit on him. Do you dig?"

"What's the point of it?"

"The point is the point."

"I thought we were friends, Bill?"

"You got no friends here," Sam told Lesser.

"Suppose I don't play?"

"If you gon fuck black you gon face black," said the light-skinned woman, Jacob's friend.

"Off the shmuck," said the flute player with flowers in his beard.

Several of the brothers nodded. Lesser felt his testicles tighten.

"I'll begin like easy so you can join the fun," Bill

said in his resonant raspy voice. "I ain't gon work on your mama and sister which is the way we do it, but come right to the tough-shit funk of it, special for you:

"Lesser, don't think you so hot,
You got the look of a shit-pot."

Some of the blacks snickered as the bull fiddler bowed a high chord.

"Now raise me on that."

Lesser stood mute.

"If you don't we might have to play a different kind of a game."

"Poker?" the writer bluffed, truly frightened.

"Man, have you lost your nuts down the can?"

The blacks laughed.

Lesser figured it was a game so long as he played it.

"Willie, your mouth is a place of excrement."

To his surprise he roused a titter of amusement.

The bull fiddler fiddled a low note.

Bill blinked in scorn, his tumid eyes momentarily refusing to focus.

"Lesser," he said, when he had got a new fix on him, "I see you runnin a bad trip. And I see that you a mammyrammer blowhard fart that has no respect for hisself."

"What good is a contest of imprecation? All it does is arouse bad feeling."

He roused raucous guffaws.

"Listen to that soft bullshit," Sam said huffily.

"Now you leave this honky to me," said Bill. "He is my guest."

More laughs.

Irene came over, her cape and hat on, leather purse hanging from her shoulder. Her long hair seemed longer.

Lesser thought if he hadn't gone to bed with Mary he might now be outside somewhere with Irene.

"Willie, can we go home now?" she said, not looking at Lesser. "I'm tired."

"Go on home."

"Couldn't you come with me?"

"Go fuck yourself."

"If I could what would you do for kicks?"

The sisters let out little shrieks of laughter and some of the brothers laughed. The bull fiddler slapped his knee. Irene retreated to the window.

"Lesser," said Bill, testily impatient, "I called you a mammyrammer blowhard fart. Don't that tempt you to return me an answer?"

"If you have to do this, why don't you write it? I thought you were a writer." Lesser's voice was hoarse, his underpants damp.

"Don't tell me what to write, chum," Bill said, raising his head haughtily. "I don't need no bleached-out Charlie to tell *me* what to write."

"Amen," said Jacob 32.

Lesser's fear incited anger. "If you have some kind

of complaint about me why don't you say it directly? Why pretend to play this stupid game? If what you want to say is none of your business in the first place, then let Sam say it."

"I told you not to let this redneck shiteater come along here," Sam complained.

Jacob 32 nodded.

"What is the answer to the words I have laid down to you?" Bill said, irritated. "How much more of a motherfuckn coward you gon be?"

"I could call you filthy prick," Lesser offered.

He saw Irene, across the room, make a gesture of silence.

"I withdraw that."

"You can't withdraw nothin," Bill said, moving his glowing face close to Lesser's. "That's the fuckn rules of it. Now isn't the reason why you want to withdraw it because it really don't say what you wanted to call me? Wasn't you plannin to say filthy nigger prick, without havin the courage to get it out? Tell the truth, man."

"I'll tell the truth—I thought of it because I know you want to hear it."

"Fine and okay," said Bill. "But now I'm gon call you a fartn shiteater faggot whore kike apeshit thievin Jew." He spaced each word slowly and ended with a hard beat.

The blacks murmured approval. The bongo player tapped out a little tune. Sam wiped a happy tear from under his eyeglasses.

"I get the message," said Lesser, "and concede the game. That's my last word."

There was a hush. The room smelled of sweat. He thought he would be struck on the head, but nobody moved. Those who continued to look on were bored. The man in the red fez yawned. The bull fiddler packed away his instrument. People drifted away. Bill seemed satisfied and Jacob 32 enjoyed a cigar.

Lesser pulled his hat and coat off a hook on the wall and headed for the door. Irene, as he went by, threw him an embittered look.

Three brothers sprang to the door to block Lesser's exit but Bill whistled shrilly and waved them aside.

"Let the white spook exit out."

The spook, whiter than ever, humiliated to the soles of his shoes but still in one piece, left the loft as Mary burst out of the bathroom and embraced Irene.

○

Down the block Lesser waited across from a broken street light, hoping Irene would walk out after him, but when she came out she was with Willie. They headed the other way. Throughout the night Lesser dreamed of her. He dreamed she had come to his room and they sat without touching because she was married to Willie. When he woke in the dark, thinking of her, from the weight on his heart he knew he was in love.

○

Bill, with a low snuffle, came in after work the next afternoon. He sat in Lesser's ragged armchair, thick hands clasped between stubby knees, gazing at the floor. He looked as though he had shrunk an inch, lost weight. His overalls hung droopy over his newly washed bulky green sweater. He adjusted his wire-trimmed glasses and smoothed the bushy ends of his Mongolian mustache.

"I sure got nothing done today, not even one lousy sentence left over to keep. Man, I have a hangover bigger than an elephant ass."

Lesser, sitting motionless, did not speak.

Bill said: "I want you to know, Lesser, that was how I saved your skin last night."

"Saved whose skin?"

"Sam wanted the brothers to beat up on you and crack your nuts for putting the meat to his bitch, but I got you in the game so they could see you get your shame that way and not want your real red blood."

Lesser said he was, in that case, grateful.

"You sure as shit don't look it."

"Take my word."

"I just wanted you to know how I did it."

Lesser afterwards thought it would be better not to know. Not to be concerned with gratitude or ingratitude. To love Willie's girl in peace and with joy.

○

Sheltered in a doorway late one afternoon, Lesser watches it snow. A black head looms out of the snow, stares at him fixedly and disappears like a moon entering a cloud bank. The black head is in Lesser's. He has been tormenting himself all day about Bill: He has little, why should I make it less? Less if he loves her, more if he doesn't—I wish I knew.

He waits in the doorway above a five-step stoop across the street from where Irene lives, in a red-brick apartment house on West Eleventh. He had gone that morning into the vestibule to look at the name on the mail box: IRENE BELL—WILLIE SPEARMINT. Harry sees a letter in Irene's box, one he has written often but not on paper. He imagines Willie reading it by matchlight.

The letter speaks of Lesser's love. Willie reads it and sets it afire with a match. Maybe he would if he were there, if the letter were there. But Willie's in his room on the fourth floor of Levenspiel's deserted house, hard at work on his new book. Lesser, since the morning after Mary's party last week, has not been able to concentrate on his writing. He walks back and forth in his room, but when he sits down at his desk he does nothing desperately and gets up.

He hadn't tried to write that morning. He had left the house early. He had walked to Fifth Avenue, caught the bus there, then cut over to Sixth. He had rung her bell. Lesser had missed Irene, gone off to a rehearsal. He had gone back home, tried to write, returned after a day of not writing. He had told himself not to go. Stay the hell away. Wait it out. This wasn't the time to be in love. Willie was a complicated guy. Lesser felt he wouldn't want a white man to be in love with Irene.

But he had left the house again to see her.

It's night. It's snowing. After a while he sees the snow. He watches it fall into the street, cover the sidewalks, window ledges, the cornices of the houses across the street. Lesser has been waiting for hours. He has to tell her he loves her or he may never write again.

A church bell faintly bongs the quarters, making the wait longer. Lesser adds up each quarter of an hour. He always knows what time it is. It is past six. At last a tallish girl in boots and cape, wearing a green wool hat dusted with snow over her blond but truly black hair, comes around the corner. Lesser watches her in the snowy light of the street lamp. He crosses the street and calls her name.

Irene looks at him as though she doesn't know him. Then she looks as though she reluctantly does.

Lesser says it's Lesser. Who else can it be?

She wants to know why he had said shalom that day, meeting her outside the museum.

"I meant don't be a stranger."

"Be white? Be Jewish?"

"Be close is better."

"What are you doing here?"

"It's a simple thing," Lesser says. "I came to tell you I love you. I figured you'd want to know. I've wanted to tell you the last couple of days but I've also not wanted to. I think you know why."

She seems not greatly surprised although her eyes are apprehensive, then moved. It's hard to tell; she is after all a stranger.

"I thought you were interested in Mary?"

"I won't say I wasn't. I slept with her for want of you. I felt jealous of you and Bill when I saw you on Lexington Avenue."

She gazes into Lesser's eyes. "Are you in love with me because I'm Willie's Jewish white girl? I mean does that have something to do with it?"

"Maybe. I wouldn't say so."

"Do you want to save me from a miserable life with a black man, an ex-criminal?"

"My love professes no more than love. Do you love him or don't you?"

"I've already told you. We talk about breaking up but neither of us makes a move. He still pits his black book against his white bitch. I see him weekends but we don't really enjoy each other. I don't know what to do. I want him to do it first."

"I love you, Irene, I want you."

"What kind of want?"

"A long want."

"Say it plainly, I'm not very subtle."

"I'd want to marry you after I finish my book."

She is moved, her hungry eyes searching his, yet smiles sourly.

"You're both alike."

"I've got to write but I've got to more than write."

Irene listens, then takes his hand. They kiss with cold lips.

"These boots leak. My feet are wet. Let's go up-stairs."

They enter the building. Irene removes her boots and dries her feet with a black towel as Lesser watches.

"Take off your coat," she says.

In the bedroom stands a double bed, a picture of a black Jesus hanging on the wall above the headboard.

"Why a black Jesus?" Lesser asks.

"Willie won't let me hang any pictures of whites. I won't hang flower pictures—I like real flowers."

"But why Jesus?"

"Rather than Rap Brown. Is there a black Moses? I believe in God."

Through the windows it is snowing heavily.

They embrace, her hands moving up his back.

"I'm afraid of what we're doing though I want to do it."

"Willie?"

"Also myself."

"I love you, you are lovely."

"I don't feel lovely. I feel off-base, off-key, dissatisfied. I'm also afraid to get involved with another writer."

"You said you were more confident about your life now."

"That comes and goes."

"You're beautiful, Irene."

"I don't feel it."

"Feel it in me."

In bed she feels it. They kiss, grope, bite, tear at each other. He licks the floral scent of her flesh. She digs her nails into his shoulders. He is aroused by their passion.

She comes as though astonished, touched by lightning, whips both legs over his back. He spurts into her.

Afterwards Irene asks, "Do I smell black to you?"

"I smell your sex. Do you feel black?"

"I feel satisfied. I still feel some guilt but I feel satisfied."

"I want you to let the blond hair grow out. Let it grow black."

"I've started already."

As they lie together, Lesser on his back, Irene resting on her side, her face pressed to his, he watches the blowing snow tinkling against the windows and thinks of Bill Spear alone in the vast empty house, writing at his kitchen table. The snow swirls in a white haze around his head.

It's a free country.

Listen, Lesser, I just wrote down this song:

I got this redhot with mustard on it
      I'm gonna eat my meat,
I got this hamburg with onion on it
      I'm gonna eat my meat,
I got this spare rib with BarBQ sauce
      I'm gonna eat my meat,
I got you in bed with nothin on you
      You gonna eat my meat.

Who's it about, Willie?

Bill, Lester, call me Bill.

Bill—excuse me.

Just me and my gal Sal. How do you like it now, gentlemen?

○

Clouds pile high over the island,
    Thunder crack them nuts,
    Lightnin run out on catfeet,
    The rain pour,
    Wind fly,
    Coconut trees bend low,
    Waves crashin rocks on the shore,
    Dead gulls gonna lay on the beach in the mornin,
    Rotten fish slop in the sea,
    Storm wake up Lesser,
    He hang onto his bed,
    Know it pitch black without tryin no light,
    He try his light,
    It pitch black,
    He run down them shadow-flyin stairs,
    Light Lucifer matches,
    Go in the cellar with a #30 fuse plug,
    When the lights turn on,
    This unknown dude layin on the cement floor,
    One leg sawed off to his knee,
    He layin in front the hot furnace,
    His pants leg bloody,
    Puddle of wet blood on the floor,
    Lesser shriek out,

Can't see no bleedin leg layin round,
He run upstairs to tell Willie,
What he done did see,
He gnawin this white bone,
What that you eatin, Mr. Bones?
Don't shit me, Lester,
I know your real voice,
What are you eating, Bill?
Breast of chicken,
White meat part,
Honest to God?
Looks like a big bone,
It's pig's foot, boy,
Kosher meat, wanna bite?

Irene moans. Lesser wakes out of unsound sleep and snaps on the bed lamp.

○

Lying in bed with her one night under the picture of the black Jesus, Lesser wanted to know when they would tell Bill.

"What do you want to tell him?"

"You know what. Either you tell him or I do, or we tell him together."

"Couldn't it wait for a while?" Irene lay with her

head in a mass of darkening hair on her pillow. She looked very lovely and it troubled Lesser that she had become apprehensive at his question, her eyes gone somber.

"Couldn't we let it die naturally?"

"It weighs on my mind."

"I'd like it better if Willie tells himself—when he tells *me* it's over. But if it actually comes to having to tell him, I'd want to do it myself."

"The sooner the better or he'll be knocking on your door on Friday."

"Would that bother you so much?"

"Wouldn't it bother you if he expected to get into bed with you? You're not his bitch any more."

"Fuck you if you use that word. It's his word, not yours."

"Whoseever word," Lesser said. "I'm not sharing you with him or anybody. Either you're committed to me or you're not."

"I'm committed to you, though I'm not all the way uncommitted to Willie."

"You wouldn't expect to go on sleeping with him while you're sleeping with me?"

"The sex part isn't what worries me right now," Irene said.

"What does?"

"For instance Willie was here yesterday."

"He was?"

"For a shower. He showered, changed his underwear and left. I was gone before he got out of the bathroom. That's how much sex there was. I sense he wants to leave me though I'll be frank and say that if he stopped writing for any amount of time he might want me again. Not that I'd be available of course. I have other fish to fry."

"Like me?"

"You know what I mean."

She reached for a comb, sat up and swept several long strokes through her hair.

"You'll have to trust me, Harry."

"I trust you."

"Sex isn't the important thing."

"What is?"

"The important thing is what happens to Willie after he leaves here. He hasn't got two nickels to rub together. How's he going to live and write? I worry about that. Willie's struggle to be a writer—from being in prison to actually writing the kinds of things he is, his stories and novel, is one of the most affecting things I know about anybody's life. It moves me an awful lot. He has to go on."

"He will."

"That's what I'm worried about. It's true he doesn't pay rent in that creepy building you're in, but he's got very little to live on—a tiny Black Writing Project grant he got in Harlem that pays him a little bread a week. He and I agreed I would help him till he got some kind of advance cash on his book, but what it's really amounted to is I've been supporting him most of the time since he moved in with me. I wouldn't want him to go back to numbers, or pushing, or anything like that."

"That's the past," Lesser said. "You're dealing with a committed writer now."

"Suppose he has to look for work, when will he find time to write? He writes slowly and needs a lot of free time. He's slower than ever since he met you."

"I don't make his choices for him."

He told Irene he had worked part-time in a factory when he was on his first novel.

"I still had plenty of time to write."

"Any factory would probably pay him half of what they paid you and expect him to do twice the amount of work."

"I worked my ass off."

"Willie'd tell them to shove it."

"Not if his writing comes first."

"I know we're not," Irene went on, "but I have this awful feeling as though you and I are a couple of Charlies giving a nigger a boot in the ass."

"I don't feel that way," Harry said. "All this amounts

to is two people—you and Willie—finally agreeing to end an affair. If you aren't betraying him as a man you aren't betraying his color. Forget the Charlie bit."

Irene nodded. "I know it's crazy, but he's been hurt so often because he's black. You've read his writing. I can't help being sensitive about it. It's one of the reasons I feel afraid to tell him about you and me, though I know he has to know."

"That's assuming he'll be hurt. You also said he mightn't be."

"I just don't know for sure. Willie's such an unpredictable man."

"So am I," said Lesser.

The telephone rang: it was Bill.

Irene put her finger to her lips. Lying beside her in the black's former place in her bed, Lesser listened to his voice on the phone.

"I won't be coming around to say howdo this Friday, Irene," Bill said tonelessly. "I was thinking I would but my chapter is down on me right now and I got to stay with it till it lets up and I got the right action moving along."

"What's the right action?"

"If I knew I wouldn't be talking about it."

Irene said she was sorry.

At the same time she gave Lesser's fingers a squeeze.

Willie was saying he'd be around in a week or two.

"I can think of a whole lot of things I like to do to you then."

"Don't depend on it," she said quietly.

After a short silence he said, "Now don't think I have stopped feeling affection for you, baby."

Afterwards Irene, her eyes uneasy, said to Lesser. "I guess we'd better tell him, but I want to be the one that does."

"The sooner the better or it might get sticky. I wouldn't want it to mess up my mood for writing."

"Oh, the hell with your mood for writing," Irene said.

She seemed about to cry but when she had shaken that off was again affectionate to Lesser, cradled his head on her breast.

○

Though Lesser had worried being in love with Irene —Willie in the wings—might complicate his life and slow down his work, it did not. Finishing his book after ten years of labor had of course to be his first concern. But mostly what happened was that he was often high on reverie and felt renewed energy for work. When passing under a leafless maple tree he thinks of Irene and a blessing descends. Then he notices its branches swollen with buds and has this livened hunger to write.

Lesser was rid of oppressive loneliness and every dirty trace of jealousy; he felt a fluent breadth to his emotions, a sense of open sea beyond, though he didn't kid himself about objective freedom in the world he lived in. Still, one was, in a sense, as free as he felt, therefore he had never been freer. Because of Irene he lived now with a feeling of more variously possessible possibilities, an optimism that boiled up imagination. Love's doing. It helped him write freely and well after having had to press for a while. And when you were writing well that was your future.

They met almost daily now, yet as though in secret, for although Bill was staying away he still had his key to her apartment and might at any time pop in. If he found them together it might go well, it might go badly. Lesser hoped it would not go badly. Irene and he met in the late afternoons, walked in West Village streets and parks, hunting signs of spring; they stopped at bars and ate in restaurants she knew. They talked of their lives from childhood and often embraced. She was not, Harry thought, truly in love with him yet, but was closer to it today than she had been yesterday. He felt she trusted him, though still not sure of herself. Lesser waited, it wasn't a bad thing to be doing while you were pushing ahead with your book. During evening rehearsals, or performances once the show had opened, he waited for her in a bar near her house. He wanted to see her act but Irene asked him not to come. Once he sneaked into the theatre and watched her in Ibsen for an act. She was better than she said; he'd thought so. She fought her way into a part and that helped the emotion. Her voice in the theatre surprised him; it was lower, stronger than he had thought. Sometimes Lesser waited for her at the movies and afterwards they went to her place to make love. Irene insisted on going up first, then buzzed the buzzer and he, releasing his breath, came up.

The writer saw little of Bill, very little, thank God, considering circumstances. The black, locked in struggle with his difficult chapter, barely surfaced. All day he typed and at night kept his smoking machine by his mattress as he slept. Sometimes when he had to go somewhere, he left the L. C. Smith with Lesser and was then in and out, hardly stopping to say a word. His face was strained, almost stricken, his tumid eyes clouded. He could barely bring himself to nod to Lesser's hello. The writer felt especially bad to be sleeping with his girl—to be in love with her—and keeping it from him whose present pain he so well understood. As though Bill's travail made him all the more victim; for this reason all the more necessary to tell him the truth, whereas, logically, considering the trouble he was having with his writing, maybe it was best to keep the news from him until he was in better shape to hear it—bad news or good.

"Still, once you tell him I'll feel a hell of a lot better," Lesser said to Irene. But she was convinced Willie would almost momentarily appear in the flat to say, "Thanks, Irene, it was real sweet but now I got plans that don't include any white chick, which I am sure you understand why." He had been in again to take a shower and had left a little note of greeting: "Hi, sugar, I took a ten-spot out of your loose change. I will be seeing you soon but not that soon as long as this crucial chapter is still acting up so bad. Chow."

After another week of not seeing him—they were into early April at last—though one of her eyes at times tended towards despondent, Irene was on the whole more relaxed; she was more easily affectionate with Lesser out of bed, as though she had proved her point: her affair with Willie Spearmint—since there was no affair where there was no Willie—had run its course and was dead on both feet; nor had there been any serious stress, rending of garments, nasty recriminations. It was best to have handled it as she had insisted, and if Willie felt like blaming anyone he had himself to blame first.

Lesser once asked her whether she missed the mood, the pitch of black life—as much as she had had of it with Willie. "Some," she said. "But I've personally gone through that bit. I see Mary once in a while"—she gazed into Lesser's impassive eyes—"but I don't really miss those who weren't my friends, though I think of some of them on and off. I liked Sam, you have to get to know him. Willie used to take me to Harlem when we first began to go together and that was like a perpetual carnival or trip all its own. But after one of the brothers had talked to him privately—I think it was Jacob—he stopped inviting me and used to go by himself. He even began to say he wasn't sure that I ever really did understand soul. That hurt me a lot and was one of the things that made me begin to have doubts."

Her hair grew in like a black cap on her blond head. Irene folded up and put away on the closet shelf the two thick black bath towels that were always adrift in the bathroom, and she took down, wrapped in brown paper, and hid, the picture of the black Jesus. Her nails had grown in; she plucked her brows thick and shaped them neatly, sometimes they looked like broken wings; she had redeemed her face, and perhaps something inside her, for she seemed kinder to herself. One day she told Lesser she had made up her mind to quit acting. "I'm not a natural. This present play is my last, I've decided. I want to really change my life. I've had enough of certain kinds of experience."

He asked what other kind.

"Well, you know most of it, and besides that, psychoanalysis. I bore myself silly at the trivia I give out. My analyst doesn't even try to hide his yawns." She said she was convinced there was little left to say. "I feel attached to him and a little afraid to be all on my own, but I really feel that it's winding towards the end." She then suggested they might want to move to some other city; she was fed up with New York. She hoped to find a job that really interested her, or maybe go back to school for a while.

"Would you consider moving to San Francisco, Harry?"

"Sure, when I'm done."

In another couple of months or even less, he thought, he would have fashioned the true, inevitable end of his novel; it was working itself out—really moving lately. Then a quick intense last correction of only such pages as needed it and done.

"Should we think in terms of three or four, or maybe five months at the latest?"

"Why not?" said Lesser.

Irene said she would write Willie a note, asking him to pick up a couple of cartons of his things she'd packed up.

"You could slip it under his door maybe? And once he gets it, then we'll have to have that talk we have to have."

"Write it and I'll slip it under his door," Lesser said.

When they were in the street, later, Irene kept glancing back as though expecting someone to catch up with them, who would say would Lesser kindly split and leave him with his bitch; but if Willie was around he was nowhere in sight.

○

One morning after knocking on Lesser's door, Bill, not really looking at him, thrust into his hand a sheaf of yellow papers, about forty. A few were cleanly re-typed but most were soiled and smeared, lines and paragraphs crossed out, with smudged interlinear rewriting, scribbling also in the margins in pencil and purple pen.

Bill's face was drawn, eyes fatigued, introspectively bleak until he focused them into strained attention through his granny glasses. His goatee and bushy mustache were badly cut, frazzled, and he looked as though he were afloat in his overalls. He swore he had lost twenty pounds.

"How's every little thing, Lesser? I keep on knocking on your fuckn door every night but nobody opens up. Are you hiding on me or really balling it now you got started again? You young bloods have got it all over us alter cockers."

He winked with weary slyness, his face burnished dry. Lesser felt a quickened heartbeat, suspecting Bill had nosed out his affair with Irene but after a minute figuring he was wrong, he hadn't. She had not yet written her letter. Lesser was still concerned that they hadn't once and for all told him. Jesus, I ought to myself, even now, this minute; then he thought, it's her picnic really. But since he had built up a relationship of sorts with Bill, circumscribed but civilized, he wished, for as long as they lived in the house he could be openly in love with Irene yet on decent terms with her ex-lover, because they were both writers living and working in the same place and faced with the same problems—differing in degree because they differed in experience.

"I've had to get out more often lately," Lesser explained, glancing at Bill's chapter in his unwilling hand. "My writing was sitting in a hole for a while. Now it's out and so am I."

Bill, listening greedily, nodded.

"You have got past your rough swampy place?"

"That's right."

Lesser sweated in holding back what he felt was the reason for his renewed good work.

The black sighed.

"Mine has been smelling up my room for a lot more time than I like to count up. This chapter that you holding in your hand, for weeks I was plowing in a garbage dump, turning up old shoes and broken scissors that other people had dumped and discarded. I was writing like Richard Wright and trying to sound like James Baldwin and that made me write things that didn't belong to me. Then when I finally raised up some of my own ideas they played dead. Also lots of people who jived around in my mind just laid down and died when I wrote them in language. Man, I don't appreciate the fright it throws on your gut when your writing won't go where you are pointing to. Or you are on your knees *begging* it. Not only does that raise up doubts if you really have a true book there; but even though you know you are well-hung and your LBJ salutes when it sniffs ass, you have these rat-face doubts are you still a man. That's no good advantage to your morale. When I open my eye in the morning and see that big typewriter machine staring at me like a motherfuckn eagle, I am afraid to sit in a chair in front of it, like the keys are teeth raised to take a bite out of my personal meat."

" 'None but the brave deserve the fair,' " Lesser said.

"Come again?"

"It's a poem."

"Black or white?"

"John Dryden, an Englishman."

"Right on, I will read it. Anyway, why I came up

here is I like you to see how this new chapter chalks up. It's on that kid you read about last time, Herbert Smith, how he grows up on his street in upper Harlem and finds he has got nothing to look forward to but more shit and stress for the rest of his unnatural life. The mother in it was giving me cramps up my ass when I tried to kill her off. I couldn't get her to die right but I wrote it like twenty more times and now maybe she's expiring the way she ought to be. After that comes some other stuff I have my doubts on because it's the first time I used that technique and don't know if I handled it right. That's what's been giving me my most trouble."

Lesser finally agreed to read it, because Bill didn't know he was in love with his girl.

Maybe his reluctance showed because Bill then said in a tense voice, "If somebody doesn't read this real fast and tell me how it's going I'll blow my mind. I was thinking of telling Irene to read it but I've been staying away from her while I was writing about my—about this kid Herbert's mama, so I could write it pure. And besides that, Irene has this shitfuckn habit of saying what I show her is good even when it ain't that good."

"How do you think it is yourself?"

"If I really knew I wouldn't ask you, I honest-to-God wouldn't. When I look at it now the words look unfriendly to me. Could you read it today, Lesser, and then we can rap it over for about a half hour?"

Lesser said he thought most every good book was written in uncertainty.

"On that—up to where the book gets real terrible to write. That's where I have to get off that trolley car."

Lesser, still in conflict, said he would read the chapter after he had finished his day's work and would then go down to talk to Bill.

"It will be a real relief to me to get this part finished off," Bill said. "I been a hermit with lead balls for more than a month and looking to pass some time with my chick. Man, she pestifies me but what a sweet lay."

Lesser did not testify.

"She's a dissatisfied chick both with herself and you if you let her, and nothing much you tell her sets her right in her self-confidence so she stops analyzing and complaining about herself, excepting what you put to her in the sack."

"Do you love her?"

"Man, that's my business."

Lesser asked no more.

"If I get to see her now depends on this chapter that you got in your hand. If you say I have it right or I'm halfways home, which I think I am, I'll goof off this weekend in her pad. But if you think it's—uh—it needs more work, and I agree with you on that, then I will lay in in my office and bang on it some more. Well, read it anyway and let me know."

Lesser poured himself half a water glassful of whiskey and gloomily began reading Willie's work.

○

Since the first chapter was good there was no reason why this shouldn't be, but Lesser resisted reading it. He considered hurrying downstairs and returning it to Bill, asking out for one reason or another, because in truth he wondered if he could judge it objectively. If I say it's good, off he trots to Irene's. Which wouldn't in itself be bad, because she would then and there have to face up to telling him what she had been unable to say before. Either she told him or they were all involved in a tougher situation than Lesser had allowed himself to imagine.

With increasing uneasiness he read the forty pages, plowing through every interlinear and marginal revision; then in a wet sweat rereading every page. In the end he groaned noiselessly and afterwards was unhappy. Though the opening pages were harshly effective, the chapter as a whole, although worked and reworked, was an involuntary graveyard.

It began with Herbert's mother attempting one night to stab the boy with a bread knife. He was awakened by her smell. When he escaped down the booming steps she stumbled into the toilet and swallowed a mouthful of lye before throwing herself out of the bedroom window, screaming in pain, rage, futility.—So the chapter opened strongly with four horrifying pages of human misery, but the remaining thirty-six, to put straight the effect of her life and death in her son's mind, went badly off. Bill took on a sort of stream-of-consciousness and heavily over-worked association. He stuffed the pipes. His rhetoric, though dealing with a boy's self-hatred and his blazing fantasies of sex and violence, became florid, false, contradicting the simplicity and tensile spareness of his sensibility. Here and there appeared insights, islands of reflection, that were original, authentic, moving, but even these he had rewritten so often that the language became a compound of ashes and glue. Part of Bill's trouble was that he was trying to foreshadow a revolutionary mentality, and it didn't always fit. Partly he was attempting in his fiction to shed an incubus—his former life. This was not necessarily bad in itself but could be bad if he insisted, and he was insisting. As a result nobody in this long section came halfway to life. At best the boy was a zombie, incapable, except fitfully, of a recognizable human emotion. His remembered mother, of past and future presence, floated around enclosed in a shallow grave with a breath-stained green glass lid. Death had leaked beyond its domain.

My God, if I say that he'll hate my guts. Why do I keep getting myself into this kind of mess with him? Who's hiring Willie Spearmint to be my dybbuk?

Lesser considered lying. After inventing and discarding several strategies, then deciding to rely on what he had had to drink and another for the road to help him improvise a better one, he ran in his stocking feet down the stairs to Bill's flat to tell him what he truly thought about the chapter before his courage gave out.

He needn't be false or evasive. They had agreed that if Bill should ask him to read any more of his work, Lesser would limit himself to matters of form and would try to suggest better ways of doing what had to be done better. And Bill, on his part, had promised to listen patiently.

He did. Lesser did: fine opening even if not entirely satisfactory chapter. More ambitious than the first, good in itself but no need of this stream-of-consciousness bit—at least not so much of it: it poured forth like lava, heavied up, gave a rock-like quality to the subjective section; which could perhaps be done better in twenty pages, possibly fewer. Lighten, ease up, cut, rework; do this and this, try this, drop maybe this and that, and you may have it more effectively in the next draft. Lesser talked coolly at first, though inwardly questioning his credentials—what made him such an authority on the art of fiction—fifteen years of writing, adding up to one good book, one bad, one unfinished? And in the last analysis could a writer tell another how to write his book? Theoretically possible, but in effect useful? useless? doubtful?—who really knows? Yet, having gone this far, he droned on, both of them sitting crosslegged on the floor, Lesser holding his stocking feet as he talked, his body swaying back and forth in pure sincerity, Bill listening patiently, studying him, nodding gravely, sagely, his swollen eyes, despite a will to objectivity, becoming pinkly glazed, his body tightening; Lesser noting this as he talked on, worrying secretly, growing dry-mouthed as he finished up with a nervous smile. He felt then as though he had just assisted in the act of tossing himself off a cliff. One thing he knew for sure: he had made a serious mistake. I should never have got into giving literary advice to the man. I should have told him about Irene and me. That's what it's all about. What a jackass I am.

Then, as though backtracking, he said, "Bill, I truly don't think I ought to fool around any more with your book. At this stage whatever you think you're doing right you ought to go on doing. As for what you doubt, maybe you ought to wait till you have a complete first draft before you decide what to change. Once you know everybody's past you'll know how to handle their future."

Bill was still nodding, his eyes shut. He opened them to say, still quietly, "I know every bit of their fuckn future. What I still like to know, outside of what you have said on the stream-of-consciousness, which I don't have to use *your way* but have to use *my way*, is have I got the boy and his mama right as far as I have gone? Are they for real, man? Don't shit me on that."

"Up as far as the mother's death," Lesser said, "but not beyond that, in his consciousness."

Rising with a weird cry, Bill flung the chapter at the wall. It hit with a crack, the yellow pages flying over the floor.

"Lesser, you tryin to fuck up my mind and confuse me. I read all about that formalism jazz in the library and it's bullshit. You tryin to kill off my natural writin by pretendin you are interested in the fuckn form of it though the truth of it is you afraid of what I am goin to write in my book, which is that the blacks have to murder you white MF's for cripplin our lives." He then cried out, "Oh, what a hypocrite shitass I am to ask a Jew ofay for advice how to express *my* soul work. Just in readin it you spoil what it says. I ought to be hung on a hook till some kind brother cuts off my white balls."

Lesser, having witnessed this or something similar before, hurried from the room.

○

Ten minutes later he pulled a hamburger in a frying pan off the flame and shut the gas. Lacing on his shoes he trotted down the stairs back to Bill's.

The black was sitting naked at his table, his head bent over his manuscript. He had on his glasses yet read as though blind. His bulky body, reflecting the ceiling light, looked like a monument cut out of rock.

Lesser, in astonishment, asked himself: self-mortification or cooling off the heated self? Maybe he compares his flesh to his black creation on paper? Or is he mysteriously asserting the power of his blackness?

"Bill," he said with emotion, "there's more to it than I told you."

"I'm quittin my writin," the black said, looking up gently. "It's no fault of you, Lesser, so don't worry yourself about it. I have decided it's no gig for a man and rots your body bones. It eats my heart. I know what I *got* to do so why don't I do it? I got to move my broke ass to get to the true action. I got to help my sufferin black brothers."

"Art is action, don't give it up, Bill."

"Action is my action."

"Forget what I said and write the way you have to."

"I got to move on."

Bill glanced at the door, then at a window, as though trying to determine his future direction.

"What more have you got to say that you didn't tell me?"

"This," said Lesser, as though he had been everywhere and there was only one place left to go. "Irene and I are in love and we're talking about getting married when I've got my book done. We thought you wouldn't care one way or the other because you had more or less broken off with her. You said so to both of us. I wish I'd told you this before."

Bill, as he reflected, began to believe. A sad and terrifying groan, a sustained tormented lament as though erupting from a crack in the earth, rose from his bowels.

"She's my true bitch. I taught her all she knows. She couldn't even fuck before I taught her."

He rose and hit his head against the wall until his broken glasses fell to the floor. His head bounced with crack and thud until the pictures on the wall were bloodied. Lesser, in anguished horror, grabbed Bill's arms to make him stop. The black twisted out of his grasp, caught him in a headlock and with a grunt slammed his head into the wall. Lesser went down on his knees, clutching his head in blinding pain. Blood flowed into his eyes. Bill, grabbing him under the arms, lifted him, and dragged him to the window.

Lesser, coming to, grasped both sides of the window

frame, pushing back with terrified force, as the black, his veins bulging, shoved forward with savage strength. The window broke and a jagged section of glass, after a day or a week, crashed on the cement of the alley below. Lesser saw himself hurtling down, his brains dashed all over. What a sorry fate for a writer. What a mad sorry fate for his book. In the sky above the desolate rooftops the moon poured a shroud of light into the oppressive clouds surrounding it. Below, a distant red light gleamed in the thick dark. The moon slowly turned black. All the night of the universe concentrated itself into a painful cube in Lesser's head.

Crying out, he jammed his heel down on Willie's bare foot. The black gasped, momentarily loosening his grip. Lesser twisted out of his sweaty armlock and they grappled, wrestled around the room, overturning the table, the typewriter crashing to the floor. The lamp fell, light rising eerily from below. They circled each other like lit shadows. Willie's eyes blazed, his breath rang like struck metal. They grunted as they fought, uttering animal noises, Willie limping, Lesser struggling to maneuver himself to the door. They caught each other again, the black pulling, Lesser shoving him off. They broke, grabbed, and were once more locked together, head to bloodied head.

"You trick me, Jewprick, got me writin so deep you stole my bitch away."

"Let's stop and talk or we're dead men."

"What's wrong is I forgot to go on hatin you, whiteshit. Now I hate you till your death."

Neither let go, Lesser trying to force Willie away from the window, as the black, with his tense bulk, legs set back to avoid Lesser's shoe, again inched him towards the broken glass.

The door shot open: Levenspiel staring in gross disbelief.

He waved both arms. "You dirty sons of bitches, I'll get a court order."

They jumped apart. Willie, scooping up some clothes, ducked around the overturned table and behind the astonished landlord vanished from the room.

Lesser sat on the floor wiping his face with his shirttail, then lay on his back, his chest heaving, breathing through his mouth.

Levenspiel, holding his hairy hand to his heart, looked down at Lesser's blood-smeared face and spoke to him as to a sick relative. "My God, Lesser, look what you have done to yourself. You're your worst enemy, bringing a naked nigger into this house. If you don't take my advice and move out you'll wake up one morning playing a banjo in your grave."

○

Lesser twice telephoned Irene as he washed. No one answered. He combed his hair over the wound on his head, changed his bloodstained shirt and hurried in a cab to her house.

When he arrived Willie had been and was gone. She was still agonized. He had come without shoes, had pulled a pair of sneakers out of one of the cartons Irene had packed, laced them on, washed, soaped his bloody bulging forehead. They had talked bitterly. He was bruised, breathless, enraged, his eyes violent. He had left her with a black eye and swollen mouth. She wept profusely, resentfully when Lesser appeared. Irene went into the bathroom to cry, flushed the bowl and came out crying. She was barefoot, had on a black brassière and half-slip, her hair piled on her head, clasped in a wooden barrette. Her mouth was crooked, her left eye black, both eyes wet and reddened from crying. Her earrings clinked crazily as she moved.

"I begged you to let me tell him," she sobbed angrily. "Why the hell didn't you at least say you were going to?"

"There was no chance, it came up suddenly."

"Shit, there was no chance. It's your goddamn pride.

You had to be the one to tell him. It's your profession to tell everybody everything. You couldn't wait."

"I waited," said Lesser. "I wait. I waited too damn long for you to tell him. You're crazy if you think he was about to leave you. It would have gone on like this for years. I had to do something."

"I know Willie. I know he wasn't happy with me any more. I know him."

"Who are you concerned about, him or me?"

"I told you I love you. I'm concerned about Willie."

"He tried to shove me out of his fucking window."

She wrung her hands.

"Levenspiel broke it up."

They held each other.

Lesser said he had read Willie's chapter and it wasn't working out. "I told him that and yet I felt I hadn't told him anything. I had to go down and say how else I was involved in his life. That's when he flipped. I'm sorry he hit you."

"He called me filthy names," Irene said. "He said he couldn't stand the sight of me. That I had hurt his blackness. He belted me in the eye and left. Then he came back for his cartons, slapped me across the mouth and left again. I locked myself in the bathroom. This is the third black eye he's given me."

Crying again, Irene went into the toilet and the bowl flushed.

"Willie doesn't like things taken out of his hands, especially by whites. He cursed you and said we had betrayed and degraded him. I told him that what had happened between him and me wasn't all my fault. Then he said he was giving up his writing. I felt terrible. That was when he hit me. This all turned out exactly the opposite of what I was hoping. I hoped he would still feel affection for me when we broke up. I wanted him to remember whatever happy times we'd had, not to leave hating me."

"Don't cry," said Lesser.

"I wish you had let me tell him."

"I wish you had."

"Are you sure you're right about his chapter? Is it that bad?"

"If I'm not I'm wrong about a lot of other things. It's a first draft, so what if he has to make changes?"

"I don't know what he'll do if he gives up writing. It makes me sick to think of it."

Lesser didn't know either.

"I just can't believe it," Irene said. "It isn't natural. The thought must frighten him. I'm frightened and I'm also frightened for you."

"Why for me?"

"I wouldn't want you to be hurt by anyone, Harry."

"Nobody'll hurt me." He hoped nobody would.

"Couldn't you stay with me for a while?—I mean live here?"

"I have my work to get on with. All my things, books, notes, manuscripts are at home. I'm close to the end of the book."

"Harry," Irene said insistently, "Harry, they could easily get at you in that creepy empty tenement. Willie's friends are very loyal to him. They could hide in the hall or on the stairs and wait until you came out. They couldn't do that here. The elevator man watches. If he saw any strangers hanging around he'd call the cops."

"Anybody who's out to get me can get me, elevator man or no elevator man," Lesser said gloomily. "They could jump me in the street at night. They could drop a brick on my head from the next-door roof—"

"All right, stop. Then how are you going to live in the same building with Willie?"

"I don't think he'll stay there now that the landlord has found his place again. But if he does and he thinks things over he'll know I felt good will to him. If we meet I hope we can get to talking like civilized beings. If we can't we're in trouble."

"Harry," said Irene, "let's get married and move either to a different neighborhood or some other city."

"That's what we'll do," said Lesser. "As soon as the book is out of the way."

Irene was crying again.

○

Suppose he were to marry her and leave the house, abandoning it to Willie? But if he moved out Willie would have little use of it. Once Lesser had gone the wreckers would descend like vultures on a corpse.

Lesser hopped off the Third Avenue bus and hurried along Thirty-first, hugging the curb so he could watch the roofs ahead and duck if a hunk of iron came flying at him.

At the door he hesitated, momentarily afraid to go up the badly lit stairs. A million stairs, five hundred dreary floors, Lesser living at the top. He had visions of a pack of rats, or wild dogs; or a horde of blacks descending as he tries to go up. His head is riddled with bullets; his brains are eaten by carnivorous birds. There are other fearful thoughts. Enough or I'll soon be afraid to breathe. He went up two steps at a time. Lesser pushed open the fire door on the fourth floor, listened intently, holding his breath. He heard waves softly hitting the beaches, shut the door with a relieved laugh and trotted quickly up to his floor.

At his door the wound on his head pained as though struck a hammer blow. He felt death had seized him by the hair. I can't believe it, I have nothing worth stealing. But his snap lock lay on the floor sawed in two. The door had been jimmied open. Crying out angrily, flailing both arms against evil, Lesser stepped into his flat and switched on the light. With a groan of lamentation he ran from room to room, searched his study closet blindly, stumbled into the living room and frantically hunted through masses of old manuscript pages, poured over piles of torn books and broken records. In the bathroom, after looking into the tub and letting out a prolonged tormented sad cry, the writer, on the edge of insane, fainted.

○

Here's this tiny accursed island.

The war canoe touches the wet shore and the three missionaries, tucking in striped paddles and holding up the skirts of their robes, hop onto the sand and beach the long bark.

The drowsy air is stirred by whispering voices, insects buzzing, muted strings, a flute in the lonely forest, woman singing or sobbing somewhere.

The Headman Minister, in voluminous black robe with leopard epaulets and hood, and the two missionaries in white robes, wearing black masks, wander from room to room of the long hut, uncovering hidden stores. They find the wrecked man's everything:

Dutch cheese, dried meat, rice, nails, carpenter's saw, jug of rum, cornbread, compasses, ink and paper.

Sitting in a triangular circle they feast on his dried goat's flesh and drink his spirits. Though not present he knows what's going on. It's that kind of day.

The Headman Minister shatters the empty crock on the ground and rises to his feet.

Bout time we start our mission. Go on and hammer up those records, Sam.

Right on, but is it civilized to break all that music?

Black or white civilized? What orientation do you have reference to?

Just plain human?

He fucked your black woman right in front of your human eye, didn't he? Was that real nice of him to do that crime?

Sam smashes up the records with a rusty heavy hammer.

Except save that Bessie Smith, a Leadbelly he has, and that old Charlie Parker I lent him.

Right on, says the Headman. Now what about you pullin down those bamboo shelves of his books, Willie? And then we will gut the pages out of them.

Willie doesn't move.

The Headman Himself, grabbing the bamboo poles, wrenches down five cracking shelves of water-stained, leather-bound volumes saved from the sea. The books fall with a crash. He kicks them with his leather boots as the printed pages fly all over the hut.

He pulls open the stuck cabinet door. A chestful of yellowed manuscripts rests on folded canvas, formerly sails.

I brought some sulfur matches. Make a warm fire.

He toasts both gloved hands.

Warm day anyway, Sam says, sweating.

Those are old books of his he wrote long ago, says Willie. Both been published.

Then it makes no nevermind if we burn them.

The Headman drags out the chest of manuscripts, lifts the box onto his bent knee, turns it upside down and pours out the papers, shaking out the bottom pages, over the torn broken books.

Make a mighty warm fire.

Willie mops his dry brow. Hot day outside.

Where's this one he's writin now?

Willie points with pale finger.

The Headman scoops up the pile of closely written vellum manuscript pages from the three-board desk in the lattice-roofed outer room. He searches through drawers and cabinets until he finds the copy of it too, lettered out neatly on yellow foolscap.

You ought to burn up both of these yourself, Willie,

on account of this cat stole your white bitch and pissed up your black book. Deprived you of your normal sex life and lifelong occupation according to the choice you made. Must feel like you been castrated, don't it? You got to take an eye for a ball it says in the Good Book.

Willie privately burns the vellum manuscript and its foolscap copy in a barrel in the outhouse, his eyes tearing from the thick smoke—some heartburn. The hot ashes stink of human flesh.

He dips his fingers into the cinders and smears a charcoal message on the wall.

REVOLUTION IS THE REAL ART. NONE OF THAT FORM SHIT. I AM THE RIGHT FORM.

He signs it NEVER YOUR FRIEND. And pukes in the smoking ashes.

○

After a night of grief echoing through the years of his life, Lesser searched Willie's office for *his* manuscript, though that wouldn't be the same thing, not a true revenge, because he had abandoned his novel; but the briefcase with the manuscript in it, or any part of the manuscript, was not there. Neither was the typewriter. The writer ran to a hardware store on Third Avenue and bought a small ax. In rage and mourning he hacked up the table and chair he had bought for the black. With brutal force he chopped at his tasseled lamp as it bled sparks, and slashed his stinking mattress to shreds. Lesser spent hours hunting from floor to floor, flat to flat, cellar to roof, for Willie Spearmint, who was nowhere around. The assassin had fled.

Lesser wandered the rainy streets, adrift without his book to write. Harry Lesser's lost labor, lost time, aching void. Nights he lay nauseated in piss-smelling hallways, sick, grieving, the self to whom such things happen a running sore. Endlessly he cursed himself for having brought home the carbon of the final draft of the book. Each week, for years, he had placed a copy of the week's work in a safety-deposit box in a bank on Second Avenue. The box also contained a copy of the first draft of the novel Lesser had been rewriting with such unutterably high expectations. Nearing the end of his last draft he had removed the carbon of it from the box to have on hand when he wrote the last word and was ready to note final corrections on both copies, one for the publishers, one for himself. Now they were ashes. He saw himself buried in ashes.

Mourning died slowly. It never fully dies for something truly loved. He read an ink-stained wet letter he found in a puddle. In it a man wept for love of a woman who had died. How can Lesser go on after the loss of his manuscript? It isn't all, he tells himself, but doesn't believe it. It isn't all, it isn't all. The book is not the writer, the writer writes the book. It is only a book, it is not my life. I will rewrite it, I am the writer. As spring flared with leaves and flowers, Lesser having cleaned up his room and restored whatever he could, began, against the will, to rewrite once again, working from a photocopy of his first draft, typing two carbons of each new page, both of which he deposited daily in the bank box. This slowed him but after a while he didn't mind. What had happened to him had happened to others. Carlyle had had to rewrite his whole *French Revolution,* the manuscript accidentally burned in J. S. Mill's fireplace. T. E. Lawrence rewrote *The Seven Pillars of Wisdom* after leaving his manuscript on a train. Lesser pictures him running after the train. It had happened countless times before. Harry figured this time it would take less than a year to rewrite the book—because he still remembered much he had reworked. He wrote down major changes to remember. He also had a thick ledger of notes for each chapter the destroyer had missed. Willie, if he could do nothing else, or more, had long ago disappeared. His empty flat resounded silence. Alas that he had ever come to this house. Irene, Lesser rarely saw just now; she said she understood. Tears came to her eyes; she had turned her back and sobbed, her hair grown black six inches down her head, the blond strands fading. Levenspiel, despite his threats, did not bother Lesser much. He had his troubles; for one, his crazy mother had cancer and was dying. He had sent the writer a special-delivery letter offering him $7,000, four thousand of it supplied by the wreckers, impatient to be at work dismembering the building. The letter had read in part, "Considering the circumstances I could get a court order to have you legally ejected for immorality and trying to burn my house, but why don't you accept my sincere offer instead and leave quietly? Be a man." Lesser carefully considered the offer before ripping it up. He listed the advantages and the disadvantages on a sheet of paper and tore that up too. True, there would be little to eat in the course of a year but he ate little anyway.

O

He sits at his desk in his daylit spacious study, more spacious than ever, typing as fast as he can. He hopes this time to do a better job than he had done in the previous draft Willie Spearmint had so heartlessly burned.

LESSER WRITES.

The skinny ten-floor house next door is being gutted, torn down floor by floor. The wreckage chutes into the green truck-size container in the street. The huge iron ball the crane heaves at the collapsing walls, and the noise of streams of falling bricks and broken wooden beams deafen the writer. Though he keeps his windows tightly shut his flat is foul with plaster dust; he sneezes in clusters all day. Sometimes his floor trembles, seems to move; he envisions the building cracking apart, collapsing in a dusty roar. Lesser and his unfinished book go shrieking into the exploding debris. He wouldn't put it past Levenspiel to blow up the joint with a long stick of dynamite and blame it on the times.

Lesser writes extra hours at night. He sleeps poorly, one eye on tomorrow morning when it's time to write. His heavy heartbeat shakes the bed. He dreams of drowning. When he can't sleep he gets up, snaps on his desk lamp and writes.

Autumn is dark, rainy, chilly. It scuds towards an early winter. His electric heater has pooped out and is being repaired. He writes in his overcoat, woolen scarf, cap. He warms his fingers inside the coat, under his arms, then goes on writing. Levenspiel provides a mockery of heat. Lesser complains to the housing authorities but the landlord resists cleverly: "The furnace is age fifty-one. What kind of performance does he expect out of this old wreck? I had it repaired two hundred times. Should I maybe install a brand new one for one lousy uncooperative tenant?"

"Let him move out and collect $9,000 cash."

The bribe has increased but this is where Lesser's book was conceived more than a decade ago, died a premature (temporary) death, and seeks rebirth. Lesser is a man of habit, order, steady disciplined work. Habit and order fill the pages one by one. Inspiration is habit, order; ideas growing, formulated, formed. He is determined to finish his book where it was begun, created its history, still lives.

A wonderful thing about writing is that you can revise, change images, ideas, write the same book better than before. Some of it already reads better than before, though not all; and Lesser is worried about the very end. He feels he hasn't conceived it as it should be. But he will, he will. There's no reason I shouldn't except that some endings are more elusive than others. As though, with them, you are secretly dealing with death although your purpose is to comprehend life, living. Some endings demand you trick the Sphinx.

Maybe I ought to write the end now and carry on up from where I left off, rise to the mountain from the plain? I might then feel secure. If I got the ending down right, as it must be, I could collect Levenspiel's bribe, move off this brick glacier and write the rest in comfort, maybe at Irene's?

Lesser has his doubts.

Sometimes the writing goes really badly. It is painful when images meant to marry repel each other, when reflections, ideas, won't coalesce. When he forgets what he meant to write and hasn't written. When he forgets words or words forget him. He types *w*ither for *e*ither all the time, Lesser sometimes feels despair's shovel digging. He writes against cliffs of resistance. Fear, they say, of completing the book? Once it's done what's there to finish? Fear of the ultimate confession? Why? if I can start another book after this. Confess once more. What's the distant dark mountain in my mind when I write? It won't fade from inscape, sink, evanesce; or volatilize into light. It won't become diaphanous, radiance, fire, Moses himself climbing down the burning rock, Ten lit Commandments tucked under his arm. The writer wants his pen to turn stone into sunlight, language into fire. It's an extraordinary thing to want by a man his size and shape, given all he hasn't got. Lesser lives on his nerve.

O

Irene said she understood, really.

She had at first been dreadfully upset, hurt at the way things were going. She had hoped her life would go more evenly, predictably, than before. "Though what Willie did to you was an outside act and I oughtn't to blame myself for it, I suppose. I mean blaming myself for not telling him we were thinking of getting married before you did. But I do feel guilty at what happened to your book. I feel awful." She was for a while moody, depressed, waked at four in the morning and for hours lay awake contemplating her life, before she fell asleep and slept late. She said she understood only too well how Harry had felt at the destruction of his manuscript, and why he was now so driven in working out this new draft of his book. She had known beforehand his nature; Willie had told her he was married to his book. She said she loved him and would try to wait with patience.

Lesser was grateful to her. Since he worked nights now he saw her weekends only. Saturday afternoon he would pack his shaving kit and a change of underwear, and move in with Irene until Sunday night. After supper Sunday he walked crosstown to Third Avenue and took the bus back to his street. As a rule she did not complain when he left. It was like life with

Willie recently, she said with an ironic laugh. But one Sunday when he was tossing his shaving things into his kit, Irene said in sudden irritation, "Really, Harry, all you do is sit on your ass writing. When you come here you sit on your ass reading."

"Not when we're in bed."

"That's the order of things. You write and read and you leave time to get laid, then you head back home. What sort of life is that for me? Why don't you fuck your book and save time all around?"

"The only way to get a book done is to stay with it. Why I read your detective stories is to turn off my writing thoughts, though just holding a book in my hand is enough to turn them back on. It's no fault of intention."

"I'm not saying the way you are is a fault. In fact I'm not sure what I'm saying, I feel that mixed up." She sighed, stroking his face with the back of her hand, "I understand, Harry, honestly. I'm sorry I'm impatient."

They embraced tightly. He said he would call tomorrow. She nodded, her eyes dry.

On the bus it seemed to Lesser that his book was a smaller thing in his mind than when he had thought of it last. But when he arrived home and flipped through the good pages he had written last week, it regained its size and promise.

Lesser sat at his desk and wrote Irene a love letter. Remembering the time of his first love for her, he tried to say honestly that although his feeling now was less intense—life flows, changes, the regularity of sex reducing desire, his book eternally in mind—in truth he loved her and wanted her love. After he posted this letter he remembered he had written much the same one last week.

Irene looked lovelier than ever. She wore tight brown boots with gold buckled straps around the calves. Or red suède boots laced with black laces; and moved with pigeon-toed grace. She wore short thick expensive skirts, embroidered blouses, and hats that looked like exotic woolen flowers. She had snipped off five inches of her blondest hair; it hung now to just below the shoulders. Her eyebrows were more thinly plucked, her pink nails long and smooth, with elongated crescents. She wore complex structures of dangling earrings she liked to look at in the mirror. She had given up her gardenia scent, then tried one new kind after another. Lesser loved to watch her dress. She dressed slowly, a cigarette held loosely in her mouth as she selected things to wear. She concentrated on dressing as she dressed. He wondered if Willie, passing her on the street, would recognize her at first glance.

Irene asked Lesser how long it would take him to finish finally and he said six months though he thought closer to ten. He didn't tell her he sometimes feared the book would fall apart before the end, a fear he hadn't had with either of his other novels. Irene said in that case she might stay on with her Off-Broadway group if they did another play, she wasn't sure. She also thought she would go on with her analysis. She had been about to terminate it but since their plans were unsettled she thought she might continue for another six months, though she felt she knew most of the important things about herself. "For one, I'm not career-oriented; I'd rather be married and have a family. Does that disappoint you in me, considering how many women are going the opposite way nowadays?"

Lesser said it didn't.

"I figure one fucking creative person in the family is enough," Irene said. She laughed self-mockingly. "What a bourgeois shit I've become."

Lesser said if a family was what she wanted, she deserved to have one.

"It's what I want but who deserves anything? Is marriage what *you* really want, Harry?"

He said it was and didn't say more. He did not add, after he had finished his book.

After Willie was gone, Irene told Lesser, she had considered moving out of her apartment, thinking he might sometime return. She felt she could not face him again after what he had done to Lesser's manuscripts. Willie hadn't given back her door key, so when she decided not to move she had had her lock changed. But he stayed away and it sometimes troubled her that she had changed the lock, as though that held some symbolic meaning she wasn't sure of, concerning herself. She was sorry she did not know where he was now and sometimes worried whether he had enough to eat. She would have liked to talk to Willie as a friend, to find out what he was thinking and doing. He had always generated excitement around him when he wasn't writing, or at least was not as worried about his work as he later became. Though in the end he had loved his black book more than he had her, Irene thought of him with warmth and affection.

"Naturally I'm attracted by characters like both of you," she said to Lesser, "men more deeply involved in their work than with me, maybe because that's the way I really want it. That's in my mind although I'm not sure and my analyst won't comment one way or another. Maybe it's because I can't do certain things I admire and want to be close to men who can. I just happen to like guys with imagination, though they can be awfully self-concerned bastards and make life more complicated than it should be."

As she spoke, her expression was restless, her eyes vague, her attempted smile neither smile nor not smile.

When Lesser's funds began to go seriously low he

limited his spending to necessities, except for movie tickets and an occasional meal out for Irene and him. But Irene, who had observed he was parting more reluctantly with a buck, insisted on lending him a few dollars when he was short of cash. Lesser accepted, provided she would let him pay her back when he got the advance on his book. He considered, as he had more than once, asking his agent to get him an advance on the basis of the first draft of his novel but decided not to; he preferred to show only finished work. He could show the section he had already completed but did not like to submit part of a novel; they might get a wrong idea what the rest of it would be like. He couldn't really tell them what it would be like until he had finished.

Irene reminded him that if he accepted the nine thousand dollars from Levenspiel he'd have it made.

"We could get married, Harry, and move to a big apartment with a quiet, well-lit study for you. What difference does it make if you write some other place than this morgue you live in? I'd keep on working and your writing would go on with lots less distraction all around."

Lesser said he had thought of that but the writing was going better now and he didn't want to interrupt the flow of it by having to pack all his things, move into a new apartment, unpack his and her stuff, and have to get used to a new place to work, as well as to a new way of life in marriage. All this would have to wait a little longer.

"I thought you were wanting more from your life than just writing," Irene said. "You said that the night we first slept together. You said you wanted your writing to be only half your life."

"I do and thanks to you I'm less uptight and not lonely. But the book, for the time being, has first priority."

"Now and forever, till death do you part. And if not this book, then the next."

Lesser, searching in one of Irene's bureau drawers for a small pair of scissors to trim the hairs in his nostrils, came across an old snapshot. It was Willie laughing at an egg in his hand, not bad looking without his stringy goatee and bushy mustache despite the eyeball prominence of his eyes. The laugh did it.

"I treated him like a man."

○

"Harry," said Irene, one late-November night as they sat at her table eating sandwiches and potato salad bought at the corner delicatessen, "tell me what your book is really about. All I know is it's supposed to be about love."

Without revealing much of the plot, Lesser said his

book was called *The Promised End,* title and epigraph from *Lear.* He said it was about a writer, a black-bearded, prematurely old thirty-five-year-old man who is often afflicted by the thought that he has wasted more of his life than he was entitled to, or essence thereof. His name, in the first draft, was Lazar Cohen. Night after night he wakes in sweaty fright of himself, stricken by anxiety because he finds it hard to give love. His present girl hasn't discovered that yet but she will. He has always been concerned with love, and has often felt it for one or another person but not generously, fluently, nor has he been able to sustain it long. It's the old giving business, he can and he can't, not good enough, too many unknown reservations, the self occluded. Love up to a point is no love at all. His life betrays his imagination.

Anyway, this writer sets out to write a novel about someone he conceives to be not he yet himself. He thinks he can teach himself to love in a manner befitting an old ideal. He has resisted this idea for years; it's a chancy business and may not pay off. Still, if during the course of three books he had written himself into more courage, why not love? He will learn through some miracle of transformation as he writes, betrayal as well as bounty, perhaps a kind of suffering. What it may come to in the end, despite the writer's doubts, is that he invents this character in his book who will in a sense love for him; and in a sense love him; which is perhaps to say, since words rise and fall in all directions, that Lesser's writer in his book, in creating love as best he can, if he brings it off in imagination will extend self and spirit; and so with good fortune may love his real girl as he would like to love her, and whoever else in a mad world is human. Around this tragic theme the story turns. The epigraph from *Lear* is, "Who is it who can tell me who I am?" Thus Lesser writes his book and his book writes Lesser. That's what's taking so long.

Irene said it was a wonderful idea and she was sure the book would be wonderful too.

○

"This is an important letter, Lesser, read it over more than once. I have found out I am a sick man, my doctor gave me warning. I have steady biting pains around my heart. Though I gave up cigars it didn't help. My family is seriously worried. Lesser, you have caused me grievous and unnecessary personal worry and misery. But I am a mensch. $10,000 is my absolute top offer. Give it your serious personal consideration. I'm giving you ample notice that I have received in the mail a bid from Tishman & Co. to take over this property for high-rise construction, and I am considering selling out to them. They'll get rid of you in one way or another, leave it to them. Don't think their lawyers are like my shtunk who couldn't get you thrown out for what you did to me. They have the means to deal with the City or send in tanks. You will get hurt more than you imagine. Save yourself the pain.

"But if I sell to them you get nothing—horseshit— and I lose out to capital instead of producing it. Think about this with due deliberation and care, not to mention whatever you have left in the way of considera- tion for other people's troubles. No other offer will be forthcoming. Take my word, I am finished with you. This is the end."

○

The building next door had become a huge hole strewn with pale broken bricks and shards of plaster giving off an acrid smell after rain. It seemed to Harry that the house, supported by air on four sides, swayed in a high wind. Cockroaches left without lodgings streamed into Levenspiel's wretched tenement to stay with relatives; also some hefty rats the writer met hopping up the stairs, sniffing as they traveled. Lesser stuffed his food into the refrigerator, canned goods and all; he often ate cold meals not to create cooking odors,

also save time. The plumbing, if not actively sabo-
taged, deteriorated further. Kitchen and bathroom
taps gave forth slender streams of rusty orange water
he washed with and drank like wine. For two numbing
days the hot water turned cold and stayed like ice as
Lesser yelled on the phone in a public booth at the
Rent and Housing Maintenance people. They advised
be patient, the landlord was ailing yet had promised to
do his best. The writer cooked up pots of hot water to
shave with and wash his few dirty dishes. For a week
the toilet wouldn't flush. After trying a few filthy ones
in the house, which also wouldn't flush, he had to pay
a dime a shot to use the subway urinal until a plumber
at last appeared.

One night he was awakened by sirens in both ears, a
fire in the apartment house across the street. Crouch-
ing in his underwear at the window, Lesser saw a
glow in a fourth-floor room but no flames. Lights went
on here and there in the building. The street throbbed
with engines pumping, squirming hoses, men running. What was burning was quickly extinguished but
left Lesser actively fearing his fear: a fire would leap
alive in the house and finish off what was left of his
literary and other remains. He saw himself fleeing
naked down the fire escape, holding to his heart his
new manuscript. Sometimes as he wrote he would picture the heavy-breathing landlord touching a match

to a rubbish pile in the cellar to see what came of it. One nervous night Lesser descended to the basement to have a look around. He searched through the cob-webbed bins and janitor's paper-strewn hollow former flat. Though he found nothing to speak of he came up tensed. The useless side of my imagination. Lesser muttered against himself for having had his phone re-moved, stupid time to be saving money. Reluctantly he ascended the stairs. Truly I hate this place. The next morning he wrote badly and had doubtful thoughts of love and marriage.

He had this crawly feeling he had been watched in the cellar. One-eyed man? One-legged? Nasty thoughts. I'd best control myself, one can make trouble for himself. If anyone was there it was some poor bas-tard who had crept in out of the night. Maybe Leven-spiel had hired a nemesis to stretch his nerves. Against the will Lesser began to search out whoever it might be. If bum or strayed hippie he would call a cop and have the cat ejected. Awful thing to do to somebody without shelter but he had to fend off distraction. Lesser considered having the door lock fixed, to con-trol immigration from the outer city, paying for the job himself. He could have the cylinder changed and send a duplicate key to his nibs, who could then not claim in court that he had been boycotted out of his building; but Levenspiel in his present state of mind might have the lock jimmied off to spite him. A loss of ten or so dollars he could not afford after the big locksmith's bill for his flat: three strong new ones plus an alarm box.

Holding the short-handled ax in his moist hand, more as warning than weapon, the writer started at the ground floor and searched each dismal flat. As he rose from floor to floor he found no one present, nothing new. In Willie's old rooms, where Lesser had looked forever out of a broken window, he was astonished to find scattered over the warped kitchen floor the remains of the furniture he had bought for the black and had, in fury and misery of loss, hacked to bits. Lesser arranged the wood into a pyramidal pile. Instinctively he once more searched the closets for some sign of the manuscript of blessed memory. Not a single page resurrected but he couldn't help looking. Much that was difficult to reconstruct in the present rewriting, sometimes impossible, he had written well in the destroyed draft—words, transitions, whole scenes he could no longer recall, squeeze his brain as he would. On the fifth floor, except for some sticks of human excrement which looked a year old, and on the sixth, he found additional nothing. No signs of life to speak of. Putting possible presence out of mind he returned to his work. It occurred to him that he ought to have searched the cellar again. For what—winter?

It is winter.

The wind wails. Lesser listens and warns it to fuck off. Cold waves lash the barren shore. On the leaden sea something's adrift he can't explain. Still suspects Levenspiel's around on one crutch, or maybe his lawyer? Is it a new prowler, smoke rising from his tracks? If I were superstitious I'd be in bad shape. He remembers, as he writes, the disjunct past, fleeting images. Death of his mother in a street accident when he was a kid. She had gone out for a bottle of Grade A milk and had not come back. Death of his older brother in the war before this war. He had disappeared, "missing in action," no sign of him ever. No last word. Still waiting in some Asian jungle for a train? Useless deaths. Life so fragile, fleeting. One thing about writing a book you keep death in place; idea is to keep on writing. An aged father he hasn't seen in years. About time I wrote him again. Once I finish up I'll fly to Chicago for a visit. He thinks, too, of Holzheimer and some of the other tenants who had lived and died in the house before Levenspiel decreed Exodus. Lesser feels an excess of unnatural fears: daily fears that the day's addition to his ms. will be stolen, snatched in the street before he can get it into the bank box; that this miserable building will fall like a wounded hippopotamus spewing forth his lost pages; or the writer will be mugged on the subway stairs and lie there unable to crawl home. There's his abandoned book on his desk being read by the room. The next day—Levenspiel swears Lesser has moved to San Francisco—the wreckers descend, with crowbars rip out the tenement's intestines, heart (where he wrote), and kick in its shell. End of book, era, civilization? Man's hasty fate?

He swears he hears stealthy footsteps in the hall, takes a bread knife out of the kitchen table drawer, foolishly flings open the door and sees no one. Was it somebody real? Negative presence as though on film? The white figure of a black man haunting the halls? He goes to Irene's doctor and is told he is suffering from a deficiency of vitamin B. He is injected at intervals, feels healthier, and writes faster.

One morning as the writer, standing in the January snow, is emptying his wastebasket into the dented rubbish can in front of the building, he discovers a barrelful of crumpled typewritten yellow balls of paper. Lesser, horror-struck, drops the lid with a clang on the can.

Willie's back, I knew in my bones.

○

Setting down his basketful of torn strips of white paper in the soft snow, Lesser in heavy cap and overcoat, holding his frosty breath, again lifted the lid and rooted around in the mass of rolled balls in the

can, unfolding some, reading quickly. Willie's typewriter, sure enough; it typed these stiff inelegant letters. One after another Lesser plucked out and unfolded twenty of surely two hundred paper balls, and
carefully arranged the crumpled sheets as well as he
could. Some pages were missing, but Willie rewrote so
often it was not hard to make sense of what he was
saying. There were notes for stories, outlines short and
long, pages of fiction barely begun, letters of exhorta-
tion to the self, pages from his old novel, pages from a
new one about a sadistic pimp and his whore. Judging
from the amount of work in the can alone, Willie had
been in the house for a couple of weeks, if not longer.
Where? Maybe he had been moving from one flat to
another. He knew I was looking for him, was he looking for me?

Afterwards, not knowing why exactly, but thinking
in terms of better know than not know, once more he
listened from flat to flat, not necessarily to confront
Willie but at least learn where he was. Lesser had to
keep things in order, make plans if necessary. Maybe
telephone Levenspiel and have the intruder bounced
to protect their property? Still—so long as he writes
he's not dangerous, or so it would seem. On the second
and third floors, Lesser, moving stealthily from door to
door, heard no one. On the third, softly pushing open
the fire door, listening with held breath to detect,

absorb every source of sensation on the floor, oppressed, he heard at last a faint typing in a rhythm he recognized.

It's Willie come back, all right. Lesser located the flat and stood, on edge, at the door. He considered abandoning the building but where would he go? Through the mess of moving now? Why should he, his novel unfinished? The book was progressing fantastically at the moment. Excellent day yesterday, eight typed pages—rare for Lesser. He sensed a breakthrough—either total recall of some of the key scenes he had been unable to reassemble, or glorious recombination of events to achieve, hopefully, a better effect than before. The right end too. Besides who's the legal paying tenant?

Why had Willie returned? Is it revenge he wants? *More* revenge? Lesser shivered in his coat. He concluded he had returned to write; he was a writer. It said so in the desperate notes he addressed to himself that Lesser had found in the can: "I have got to write better. Better and better. Black but better. Nothing but black. Now or never." He had come back to the house because he had no money for rent anywhere else. Maybe he had returned in order to finish the book begun here? A man liked to stay in place when he was writing a book. You did not want to change around when you were so deep into something.

Lesser worked later that night, later most nights thereafter. Sometimes he stopped to listen, wondering if Willie had stolen up the stairs and laid his envious ear against the door to hear the writer jive-typing away.

○

He read what the other discarded in the garbage. Lesser emptied his wastebasket in the cans across the street so that Willie wouldn't see his work.

For a while Willie was rewriting the disastrous last chapter of his novel about Herbert Smith and his mother. The boy is fifteen and on hard stuff, stealing steadily to support his habit. The mother is a lush, smelly, wasted, unable to stay sober for an hour a day. Once in a while he comes to her room to cook up a fix; or sleep on the floor as she snores on her urine-wet mattress. The suicide is omitted. She dies unattended, of malnutrition, as Herbert jerks off in the hall toilet. When his mother is buried in her pauper's grave nobody's there to pretend to mourn. The next day the boy appears at her raw graveside and tries to work up an emotion. He tries to imagine her feelings about her life but soon gives up on it. Sick for a fix, he leaves, but on looking back from the fence, sees a white Jesus standing by her black grave. The boy runs back to shoo the fatass dude away.

This part of the chapter was excellent but that was as far as Willie had gone. Maybe he hadn't faced up to the rest. Maybe he couldn't.

He had written several drafts of a weird, disturbing story entitled "Goldberg exits Harlem." A Jew slumlord in a fur-collar coat, come to collect his bloodmoney rents, is attacked in a dark hall by three old men and a Jamaican woman. The Jew struggles and cries out but they stab him until blood spurts from his nose, then drag his fat body down the stairs to the cellar.

"Let's cut a piece off of him and taste what it taste like," says the old man.

"He tastes Jewtaste, that don't taste like nothin good," says the Jamaican woman.

They remove Goldberg's stabbed clothes and leave his body in the cellar.

Then they go to a synagogue late at night, put on yarmulkes and make Yid noises, praying.

In an alternate ending the synagogue is taken over and turned into a mosque. The blacks dance hasidically.

Willie had written the story at least four times but it hadn't worked out the way he wanted. After another week he was still trying.

He then wrote some experimental pages, one entitled "Manifested Destiny." This went.

black, white, black, white, black, white, black, white,
(go to bottom of page)
black, whit, black, whit, black, whit, black, whit, black
(go to bottom of page)
black, whi, black, whi, black, whi, black, whi, black,
(go to bottom of page)
black, wh, black, wh, black, wh, black, wh, black, wh,
(go to bottom of page)
black, w, black, w, black, w, black, w, black, w, black,
(go to bottom of page)
black black black black black black black black black
black black black black black black black black black
(make two pages)
BLACKBLACKBLACKBLACKBLACKBLACKBLACK
BLACKBLACKBLACKBLACKBLACKBLACKBLACK
BLACKBLACKBLACKBLACKBLACKBLACKBLACK
BLACKBLACKBLACKBLACKBLACKBLACKBLACK
(make five pages of this)
BLACKNESSBLACKNESSBLACKNESSBLACKNESS
BLACKNESSBLACKNESSBLACKNESSBLACKNESS
BLACKNESSBLACKNESSBLACKNESSBLACKNESS
BLACKNESSBLACKNESSBLACKNESSBLACKNESS
BLACKNESSBLACKNESSBLACKNESSBLACKNESS
BLACKNESSBLACKNESSBLACKNESSBLACKNESS
BLACKNESSBLACKNESSBLACKNESSBLACKNESS
BLACKNESSBLACKNESSBLACKNESSBLACKNESS
BLACKNESSBLACKNESSBLACKNESSBLACKNESS
(This is the rest of the book).

There were some short poems related to "Manifested
Destiny":

White has no glow
No light for white;
Black is true glow
Is lit from in.

I love you
Black Woman,
Touch me
To Love,
Make me
ALL BLACK

Lesser found three variations of a love poem to Irene. He had no idea whether these or "I love you/ Black Woman" had been written first.

1.

Irene
Lost Queen
I miss
To be between
Your
Jelly Roll

5.

My bitch was born white
No fault o mine
I am black night
No fault o mine

This chick I used to fuck
Now I fuck my luck
No fault o mine

6.

Irene
White Bitch
You ditch
Black Knight
Willie fuck
His luck
Howdo
Sadeye Blues

Lesser gave up poking around in the can in the snow.

○

Here's this double wedding going on, that's settled in his mind.

The old tribal chief, the marriage guardian, holding the dying goat, four quivering legs in two big hands, grunts as he lets the thick blood pour from its cunt-like wound over the threshold of his long hut. That fixes it with the spirits. Blood won't make it kosher but the white bride, dark, Jewish, beautiful, isn't really orthodox. Anyway, it's a broad threshold and a lot of red blood.

On this cool tropical summer's morning the white-haired, black-eyed skinny chief, wearing a goatskin cap with an eagle feather on his toothless head, had neatly slit the throat of the noisy he-goat for his son's daughter—the ill-starred gent who went off to America against the advice of the oracle of the Hills and Caves. He died in his blood, stabbed in chest, stomach and kidney in a Boston crap game.

"Feh," says a voice in the rear.

"Sha," says his son.

Both brides had been merrily delivered to the wedding hut by a procession of kinsmen, neighbors, and a few curious strangers. The girls of the clan, oiled and ornamented, had chanted poems along the dusty forest path, to the music of gongs, small drums, and an iron flute played by a cripple, as the sweaty youths, holding long spears, leaped and yelped as they danced, their man-meat swinging like grapes in bunches in their loincloths.

In the direction of the horned daylight moon a slender river moves to the sea in an arc from the restless ocean. The young men stack their spears against the thatched roofs of the huts surrounding the grassless courtyard. The fowl go crazy in the crowd and peck at people's feet. An old man kicks at a rooster. A dry inland wind blows in the ripe stench of cow dung.

"Feh."

"Sha."

A small brown man with scrofulous face and hands, skin like curdled milk, the chief's interpreter for the wedding, who had once in the dim past worked as a librarian's assistant in Whitechapel, says the smell is a good sign. The omen is of plenty.

"Plenty of what?" Willie asks.

"The cow which do not eat do not make excretions."

Kinsmen and wedding guests crowd into the windowless homestead, hazy with smoke from the grass fire. The notables of the tribe in soft caps and brightly colored robes sit on their carved wooden stools. Some of the elder tribesmen roll out goatskin mats and seat themselves crosslegged, puffing pipes and talking cows. They sneeze on snuff. The older wives, wearing ivory ornaments and beads, give high-pitched directions to the younger women as they prepare the chicken and yams and pour out calabashes of beer. Against the musty sides of the long hut the young men and girls lay laughing plans for later in the grass. It's a good time for almost all. The visitors from the distant country, relatives and friends of the white bride and bridegroom, of varying moods and dispositions, eye each other and wait.

The marriage guardian, his indigo toga knotted over his bony left shoulder, sits with the interpreter, their backs to the wall, as the nervous rabbi in grizzled beard and black fedora, stares in amazement at the assemblage. One bridal couple is seated before the toothless chief, the other stands with the rabbi mopping his dry brow with a gnarled handkerchief. Lesser and Mary, wearing less than most, are sitting on a leopard skin. He rubs his arms briskly, goose-flesh despite the fire on the platform that illuminates the long hut. Willie, dressed to kill, sports a black velvet hat and embroidered yellow tunic over his newly washed overalls. Irene, immaculately groomed, her thick black hair drawn in a bun over her left ear, has wound a flowered scarf around her head. She wears long golden earrings and carries a bouquet of white irises and daisies. The rabbi under the silk wedding canopy, held up by split triangular poles of quartered eucalyptus exuding an aromatic sap, is ill at ease but ready for business. He's a middle-aged Litvak, a stocky man in mud-spotted trousers that drip over dried muddy heels. His smoker's nails are soiled yellow, his beard is in disorder, his expression dazed. With furrowed brows he reads the marriage contract over and over, then nearsightedly reads it again.

The chief speaks in a guttural voice to the scum-skinned man at his side and the interpreter's words rise high-pitched to Lesser and his bride. She seems calm but he sees her hard heartbeat under her breast.

"He say. 'When our black daughter marry the white mens we do not rejoice but this is less so bad than if our sons marry so, for then a white woman will turn a man's face from the village and his kinsmen.'

"He say. 'My daughter's father, my own son, he is among the deads. So he ask me to speak with his voice, and so he give her to this white man to marry her. This be of her wish. The bride price, you bring ten cows, do be paid and we make acceptance. I have told this to the wedding gods and say to the shades of my ancestors that she be married before the people of the tribe, not with shame or hiding. The cows are not sick, they are fat, you did not cheat us.' "

The old chief, holding Lesser's image in both black eyes, nods.

" 'Our daughter will live with you and cook your food and rake your garden if you plant it for her. And she will born a manchild to carry on your lineages so your name and presence will remain here on this earth after you die. She will please your heart and you must treat her with kindness.' "

The bridegroom, in a smoked raffia skirt from waist to knees over his jockey shorts, promises he will. He is wearing the string of green and violet beads Mary Kettlesmith once gave him, a blood-red goatskin cap, and now holds upright a tall rusty spear.

His bride, holding in her hand a purple feather,

says she will be kind. Her silken hair is trimmed with small blue flowers and her legs have been rubbed with camwood. A red necklace, hung in three coils, descends between her succulent breasts. Under a short maternity skirt her stomach is in flower.

"You are married now," the interpreter says, "yet so by our customs the wedding is not done till when the first child be borned."

"It's a long wedding," says Lesser.

"You had your choice," says Mary.

Who has choice? What am I doing so far from my book I have to finish? Why am I giving spades to fortune? What you don't know who will tell you?

The chief speaks again:

" 'I am old man of many weathers and you be young. You know more book but I be wiser. I have lived my long life and know what did happen. Well, I have had six wives and twenty-nine childrens. I have oftentimes sat with death and do know the pain of many losses. Listen to my words.' "

Lesser, afraid not to, listens hard.

"He say. 'When the evil spirit try to climb in your eye keep it shut till he fall asleep.' He say. 'Do not push your spear in the belly of them which is not your enemy. If somebody do bad it do not die. It live in the hut, the yard, and the village. The ceremony of reconciliation is useless. Men say the words of peace but they do not forgive the other. He say if you be sure to remember his words.' "

"Tell him I understand."

"He say you will understand tomorrow."

The old chief's eyes fasten more tightly on Lesser's. He listens harder.

"He say. 'The darkness is so great it give horns to the dog.' He say. 'The mouse which thinks he is the elephant will break his back.' "

"I get it."

"He say tomorrow."

"Anyway I'm listening."

"He say to you. 'Eat the fruit where you do find it. The tiger which tear his gut do not digest his food.' He say to you. 'Enjoy your life for the shades paddle the years in swift boats, they carry the dark. Pass on my wisdom.' "

"I will. I'm writing a book."

"He say he do not wish his words to be in your book."

Lesser stands mute.

The chief rises. " 'Go well, you and your bride.' "

Released from his gaze, the bridegroom rises relieved.

The interpreter yawns.

The chief drinks from a gourd of palm wine.

A youth drums a hand drum.

The writer, enjoying life, shuffles into a barefoot dance with his spear. The tribesmen clap in rhythm. Lesser's raffia skirt rustles, his ankle bands clink as he thrusts his spear this way and that to drive off any lingering unclean spirits. He grunts as he lunges.

When the dance is done his poor father, A. Lesser, once a healthy tailor, now skin and bones, an irritable old man in a tubular aluminum wheelchair, says to his sweating son:

"You should be ashamed to dance like a shvartzer, without any clothes on."

"It's a ceremonial dance, papa."

"It's my own fault because I didn't give you a Jewish education."

The old man weeps.

The groom speaks to his pregnant bride. "Mary, I'm short of love in my nature, don't ask me why, but I'll try to give you your due."

"What's in it for you, Harry?"

"I guess the kind of person you are. The rest I'll know later."

"Okay now."

They kiss.

"Okay," says the scrofulous interpreter.

The rabbi intones a prayer in Hebrew.

The tribal talk subsides.

Irene and Willie, under the white silk canopy, sip

imported Mogen David from their glass goblet. The bridegroom's parents, white bones in black graves, can't make it back to the old country today; but Sam Clemence, a witness from Harlem U.S.A., despite a bad case of the runs and that he suffers intense feelings of personal loss, stands up for his friend Willie.

Irene's father, mother, and younger sister, a genuine blonde, are bunched together at the side of the canopy. The father, David B. Belinsky, a man with florid face and uneasy feet, in black homburg and silk suit, striped shirt and big tie, manufactures buttons. He smiles stricken. The tall mother sits home all day; she wears a plain white dress, orthopedic shoes, and a blue cloche hat that hides her eyes. Half her nose is visible. The saddened sister is the wife of a successful insurance broker, home minding the business and three small children.

Though the old chief's long hut is not a ship they all look seasick.

The bridegroom, after twice thoroughly searching his pockets, says he guesses he has forgotten to bring the wedding ring. All stare in astonishment. The father breathes momentarily easily but the rabbi says it is permitted to give the bride a coin instead, so Willie passes her a warm dime out of his pants pocket which Irene holds tightly in her palm during the ceremony.

The second time round—the first he listened intently to the words, Willie slowly recites after the rabbi, "Hare at mekudeshet li betabaat zu, kedat moshe veyisrael."

"What am I saying?" he asks Irene.

"I told you: 'Behold thou art betrothed to me with this ring in accordance with the Law of Moses and Israel.'"

Willie wets his dry lips. "That just for the wedding?"

"For as long as you like. You said we'd get married if we had the wedding here."

He nods and they kiss.

The guests shout, "Ya."

The rabbi recites the seven benedictions.

Willie, with two bangs of his boot, crushes the wine goblet.

"Mazel Tov," says Lesser.

The musicians pat and thud their drums, lightly, gayly. A bamboo flute sings.

"Now you are man and wife," says the rabbi. "I feel like crying, but why should I cry if the Lord says, 'Rejoice!'

"Willie and Irene, listen to me. Oh, what a hard thing is marriage in the best of circumstances. On top of this what if one is black and the other white? All I am saying is the world is imperfect. But this is your choice and I wish you health and happiness and the best of circumstances for you and your children. My rabbinical colleagues will criticize me strongly for performing this ceremony, I know this, but I asked myself would God let me do it, so I did it.

"Willie and Irene, to enjoy the pleasures of the body you don't need a college education; but to live together in love is not so easy. Besides love that which preserves marriage is that which preserves life; this is mutual trust, insight into each other, generosity, and also character, so that you will do what is not easy to do when you must do it. What else can I tell you, my children? Either you understand or you don't.

"I also ask you to remember that a wedding is a covenant. You agree to love each other and sustain your marriage. I wish to remind you of Abraham's covenant with God, and through him, ours. If we stay covenanted to God it is easier to stay covenanted each to the other."

"I will," says Irene.

"Ain't no god been in my house or ever was," Willie says. "Like what color is he?"

"The color of light," says the rabbi. "Without light who sees color?"

"Except black."

"Someday God will bring together Ishmael and Israel to live as one people. It won't be the first miracle."

Willie laughs, cries, then stands mute.

"Let's dance," says Irene.

The guests, including the notables, rise, lift their feet, and dance. Some of the youths try to imitate the newly married couples shaking their hips and shoulders but give it up and break into a stomp, shake, and whirl. The women serve a feast of chicken with sesame and tomatoes, roasted yams, and palm wine. Some of the girls, wearing flowers in their hair, dance in a circle. The black youths whoop and shout as they whirl around them.

Those who feel like crying, cry. A wedding is a wedding.

Irene asks Lesser, as they dance a last dance together, "How do you account for this, Harry?"

"It's something I imagined, like an act of love, the end of my book, if I dared."

"You're not so smart," says Irene.

THE END

○

Lesser lifted the lid of the garbage can and a hot ordurous blast thickened his nostrils. He stepped back as though struck in the face. "A dead rat," he muttered, but all he could see was a mass of crumpled blue paper balls—Willie had run out of yellow. Holding his nose he approached the can. Standing away from it, he unfolded and put together several pages from at least three pieces of writing Willie was currently working on:

In this story, on a hot summer evening as supper smells of cabbage and spare ribs linger in the shimmering air outside the tenements on 141st Street near the river, four black men station themselves on four soft-tar rooftops along the street—two on either side: they stand in an uneven quadrangle. The people on the stoops fold up their chairs and quickly move inside. A blue Chrysler drives up and stops at the curb. The brothers on the roof open fire from four directions at the uniformed black cop getting out of his new car. Two of the bullets strike him in the belly, one near the spine, and one in the right buttock. The cop spins around waving his arms as though trying to swim out of an undertow but is dead as he sits on the bloody sidewalk, staring without sight at a pigeon coop on a deserted rooftop. The story is called "Four Deaths of a Pig."

Lesser found a protest Blues song Willie had knocked off apparently in one draft, "Goldberg's Last Days," also called "The Goldberg Blues":

Goldberg, and Mrs. Goldberg, goodbye goodbye
　　All your life you been cheatin us poor black
　　Now we gon take that gold pack off your back.

Goldberg, and Mrs. Goldberg, goodbye goodbye
> Your day is gone past
> You better run fast.

Goldberg, and Mrs. Goldberg, goodbye goodbye
> Comin a big U.S. Pogrom
> Well, I'm gonna sing and hum.

He had signed it "Blind Willie Shakespear."

Related to this was a piece called "The First Pogrom in the U.S. of A." In it a group of ghetto guerrillas in black leather jackets and caps decide it will help the cause of the Revolution to show that a pogrom can happen in the U.S. of A. So they barricade both ends of a business block, 127th Street between Lenox Avenue and Seventh, by parking hijacked trucks perpendicularly across both ends of the street. Working quickly from lists prepared in advance, they drag out of a laundromat, shoe store, pawnbroker's shop, and several other kinds of establishments owned by them on both sides of the street, every Zionist they can find, male, female, and in-between. There is none of that Hitler shit of smashing store windows, forcing Zionists to scrub sidewalks, or rubbing their faces in dog crap. Working quickly in small squads, the guerrillas round up and line up a dozen wailing, hand-wringing Zionists, Goldberg among them, in front of his Liquor Emporium, and shoot them dead with pistols. The guerrillas are gone before the sirens of the pigs can be heard.

Willie had rewritten the pogrom twelve times, Lesser gave up searching for more of it. In one draft, some of the black clerks try to protect their former bosses but are warned off by shots fired in the air. One of them who persists is killed along with the Zionists. As a warning to Uncle Toms he is shot in the face.

There was a penciled note at the bottom of the last page of the story, in Willie's handwriting. "It isn't that I hate the Jews. But if I do any, it's not because I invented it myself but I was born in the good old U.S. of A. and there's a lot of that going on that gets under your skin. And it's also from knowing the Jews, which I do. The way to black freedom is against them."

O

Fog seeped into the building, filling each empty floor, each freezing room, with deadwater smell. A beach stank at low tide. A flock of gulls, wind-driven in a storm, had bloodied the cliff and lay rotting at the foot of it. The hall lights, except on Lesser's floor, were out, bulbs smashed, stolen, screwed out of their sockets. The dirty stairs were lit at descending intervals by bulbs shedding watery light. Lesser replaced the burned-out ones but they did not last long. They shone like lamps on an ocean front on a wet night. No one replaced the dead bulbs on Willie's floor.

One night Lesser, hearing footsteps as he trod down the stairs, glanced into the stairwell. In the dim light he caught sight of a black man with a thick full beard, wearing a spiky Afro like a dangerous plant on his head. Or helmet of Achilles. He looked for a moment like an iron statue moving down the stairs. Lesser's heart misgave him and he stopped in his tracks. When he gazed with eyes carefully focused the man was gone. Frightened imagination? Optical illusion? Could it have been Willie? Lesser hadn't got a good view of his face but was certain the black had held in his hand a glittering instrument. Razor? Knife? Civil War saber? Against what atavistic foe? Not me: if it was Willie he's had his revenge—more than revenge —destroyed my best creation. Reversing direction, Lesser hurried up to his room, hastily unlocked three locks with three keys, checked his dusty manuscript as a matter of course, then searched for something to protect himself with if he had to. He opened the closet door, the ax hung on its hook. He laid it on his desk by the typewriter.

Agitated, hungering to know was it Willie or was another black living in the house—a gang of them? —he crept stealthily down to Willie's floor. His door was open, a shaft of shadowed yellow light falling into the pitch-dark hallway. Who's he expecting? Elijah?

Inspiration? Pok pok pok. Son of a bitch, what's he writing now? Boy murdering his mother? Or who dies in what pogrom?

Willie, in six-inch Afro, his bulky green sweater pulled on over patched overalls—Ecce Homo!—his thick back to the door, sat on an apple box, furiously typing on the L. C. Smith atop an upended egg crate.

Hey Bill, Lesser thought in the hallway, moved by the sight of a man writing, how's it going?

You couldn't say that aloud to someone who had deliberately destroyed the almost completed manuscript of your most promising novel, product of ten years' labor. You understood his history and possibly yours, but you could say nothing to him.

Lesser said nothing.

He tiptoes away.

Maybe Willie ascends to his locked door and listens to him at work. This is no rat listening to food, this is a man, a writer himself, best at stories, Bill Spear. What's he listening for? To find out if I have survived? He listens for the end of my book. To hear it. To learn that I have, despite certain misfortunes, impediments, real tragedy, finally achieved it. He wants to believe I have—has to—so he can go on with his pockitying. Finish a book of his own—whatever. He lacks belief in his work and listens to mine for the promised end. If Lesser can make it, then so can he.

But what he listens for I am unable to construct. If his ear is sensitive he hears degrees of failure. Maybe he listens with evil ear, fingers crossed, to hinder me doing what he can't? He could be witching my nail cuttings or crooked hairs caught in a broken comb he found in the garbage can. He wills I crack, fall apart, wither. He listens for, imagines, craves to create, my ultimate irreversible failure.

○

One winter's night they meet on the frigid stairs. Darkness seeps up from the lower floors. It's Willie all right, though he looks taller, thinner, his face knobby, his kinky hair standing on end. It's Lesser, growing a limp Leninesque goatee crawling with fright. Willie's going up, Lesser, ready to spring if he is sprung at, on his way down. They stare at the other, listening to him breathe, their discrete white breaths rising in the cold. Willie's swollen eyes are the color of black paint, his sensual lips hidden by thick mustache and finely woven beard. His stubby, heavy-jointed fingers ball into huge fists.

Lesser, raising his coat collar, intends to squeeze by the black in silence, sees them, mutually repelled, drawing aside to let each other pass.

Instead, suppressing hatred, he makes a breathy effort:

"I forgive you, Willie, for what you did to me."

"I forgive you for forgivin me."

"For burning my book—"

"For stealin my bitch I love—"

"She made her free choice. I made mine. I treated you like any other man."

"No Jew can treat me like a man—male or female. You think you are the Chosen People. Well, you are wrong on that. *We* are the Chosen People from as of now on. You gonna find that out soon enough, you gonna lose your fuckn pride."

"For God's sake, Willie, we're writers. Let's talk to one another like men who write."

"I dig a different drum than you do, Lesser. None of that fuckn form for me. You hurt my inside confidence with that word. On account of you I can't write the way I used to any more."

Eyes glowing, he rushes headlong down the stairs.

Lesser goes up and tries to write.

Nothing comes of it. A faint unpleasant odor rises from the paper.

○

Lesser is afraid of the house, really afraid. Familiar things are touched with strangeness. Green mould on a pencil. A broken pitcher, standing, breaks apart. A dry flower falls to the floor. The floor tilts. A cup he drinks from he cannot recognize. A door opens and bangs, opens and bangs. He tries half the morning to find it and can't. Levenspiel banging? As though the house has grown larger, leavened a couple of useless floors, made more empty rooms. The wind, weird sad sea music, lives in them, moving through the walls as through trees in the woods. It sings above his head. He listens as he writes. Lesser writes "the wind is gone" but hears it still. He is afraid to leave his room, though sick of it, lest he never return. He goes out rarely, once a week for a bag of groceries. Sometimes when he dozes over his work he gets up to trot in the hall for exercise. Otherwise he writes.

Rereading the words he sees scenes he hasn't written, or thinks he hasn't. Like when Willie plants a lit match in a box of oily rags in the cellar and a roaring tree of fire bursts into bloom, its flaming crown rising through each melting floor. Lesser to save his manuscript—it's been weeks since he has deposited his new pages in the bank box—rushes to the fire escape. The window is blocked by thickly interwoven branches of crackling flames, heavy flaming fruit. Lesser flees to the roof. Around him long spark-filled plumes of smoke, horns of glowing ashes, ascend to the reddened sky. Masses of burning houses in a forest of fires. From close by, like the sound of waves breaking, rise a muted roaring, screaming, sobbing. Who cries there? Who dies there? Riot? Pogrom? Civil War? Where can I run with my paper manuscript?

Lesser writes. He is writing this book about love. It's his need and he must. All he has to do is imagine it to its unforeseen end as he puts the words down on paper. Irene has left for San Francisco. She wrote him a note goodbye, enclosing no address. "No book is as important as me," she wrote. With or without her he has to finish, create love in language and see where it takes him, yes or no. That's the secret, you follow the words. Maybe this man in the book will learn where it's at and so will Lesser. Although if you have to make a journey to track love down maybe you're lost to begin with. No journey will help. Yet better look for something than just not have it. The looking is the having, some say. He'll know for sure when he finishes the book. What a shame, he had written it so well in the draft Willie burned. It seems to him he understood it better than he does now despite the double thought, double labor expended. It was a good book to its about-to-be-end. He remembers almost everything in it but can't get it down again as he had it there. How can one write the same thing twice? It's like trying to force your way back into yesterday. All he would have had to do was reach out a hand, the words flow out of it.

I had only to write the last scene and spring the final insight. It would have come, completed the fiction, freed it from me, freed me. Freedom favors love. I'd've married Irene and gone to San Francisco. It wouldn't have been a bad life with her. She respects my work. We might have made it together.

He sees himself sitting in his room forever trying to finish his book as it should be done. If only Willie hadn't destroyed both copies of the manuscript. If only one had survived. He sees it clearly, every word in place. Mourning his lost manuscript Lesser rose from his desk, in misery, enraged. Snatching up the ax, he ran down the stairs, two at a time. He pushed open the fire door and strode silently up the hall. Hearing Willie typing, Lesser, alternately moved and nauseated, stole into a flat across the hall. He hid there, in states of anticipation and gloom, until the black left for coffee, or maybe he had run out of blue paper. Lesser entered his room, read the sheet in the carriage—nothing memorable—ripped it out. Then blow by blow, his eyes exuding damp, he hacked up Willie's typewriter. His blows made a clanging music. He chopped the machine till it was mangled junk. It bled black ink. The ax survived with jagged broken blade. Though Lesser shivered feverishly, he felt for a while an extraordinary relief. He did not care for what he had done; it sickened him deeply, but for a while he thought the writing might go well thereafter.

○

Lesser, unable to sleep nights, from his window on the sixth floor watches Willie, at dawn, poking into the garbage cans across the street. He had day by day been putting together Lesser's torn strips of white paper to see how his book was coming. For weeks there has been nothing in the can, but Willie still searches. Spring is coming. There is nothing in Levenspiel's deep-dented can either, no crumpled balls of blue paper written by hand. The cans are emptied twice a week, wordless.

The landlord, ill, pale, bad-breathed, began to cover up the door frames on the first floor with sheets of tin. With long nails he hammered them down. A month after finishing the first floor he began to nail the tin over the second-floor door frames. Good, thought Lesser, I'll soon be rid of Willie Spearmint. Either he'll be fenced in, unable to get out; or fenced out, unable to get in. Once he stops haunting this house I'll get my work done.

○

The writer was nauseated by not writing. He was nauseated when he wrote, by the words, by the thought of them.

Each morning, nevertheless, I held the fountain pen in my hand and moved it along the paper. It made lines but no words. A great sadness came on me.

○

They trailed each other in the halls. Each knew where the other was although the terrain had changed. The trees in Holzheimer's room had moved off the walls onto the dank floors in the flat. Taking root, they thickened there and spread into the hall and down the stairs, growing profusely amid huge ferns, saw-toothed cactus taller than men, putrefying omnivorous plants.

One night Willie and Lesser met in a grassy clearing in the bush. The night was moonless above the moss-dripping, rope-entwined trees. Neither of them could see the other but sensed where he stood. Each heard himself scarcely breathing.

"Bloodsuckin Jew Niggerhater."

"Anti-Semitic Ape."

Their metal glinted in hidden light, perhaps star-light filtering greenly through dense trees. Willie's eyeglass frames momentarily gleamed. They aimed at each other accurate blows. Lesser felt his jagged ax sink through bone and brain as the groaning black's razor-sharp saber, in a single boiling stabbing slash, cut the white's balls from the rest of him.

Each, thought the writer, feels the anguish of the other.

THE END

O

Mercy, the both of you, for Christ's sake, Levenspiel cries. Hab rachmones, I beg you. Mercy on me. Mercy mercy